Praise for Cara Hoffi

"One should not pick favorites, bu. . . . ., ..., ..,, ... Hoffman is my favorite living American writer. In her latest work, *RUIN*, each story is a wild universe driven by its own purpose, filled with terrifying elegance and ecstatic harm. I never wonder why what she's telling me matters. Brilliant and anti-redemptive, she traces the desire of her characters with surgical dexterity, each red line exposing life."
—Vanessa Veselka, author of the National Book Award–nominated *The Great Offshore Grounds*

"Hoffman writes with a restraint that makes poetry of pain."
—*The New York Times Book Review*

"Tough, scarred, feral and sexy. The book and the characters refuse to conform, and like in all good outlaw literature [Hoffman] takes sharp aim at the contemporary culture's willingness to do so."
—Justin Torres, author of *We the Animals*

"Hoffman maps the atmosphere of paranoia that descends on a formerly tranquil town as she moves deftly between its inhabitants."
—*The New Yorker*

"Hoffman writes like a dream—a disturbing, emotionally charged dream that resolves into a surprisingly satisfying and redemptive vision."
—*The Wall Street Journal*

"Beneath the deceptive lyricism of her prose, Cara Hoffman has long shown a healthy fascination with upending the social order. . . . Her observations have the keen immediacy of lived scenes, similar to drawings sketched from life."
—*Seattle Times*

"Mesmerizing."
—*New Orleans Times Picayune*

"The stories in *RUIN* deftly display the horror and ugliness of our culture of violence and consumption, yet also reveal the delicate humanity within our collective yearning. Reading Cara Hoffman's fiction makes me not only want to write better but to be better."
—Paul Tremblay, author of *A Head Full of Ghosts* and *The Cabin at the End of the World*

"*RUIN* is a collection of ten jewels, each multifaceted and glittering, to be experienced with awe and joy. Cara Hoffman has seen a secret world right next to our own, just around the corner, and written us a field guide to what she's found. I love this book."
—Sara Gran, author of *Infinite Blacktop* and *Claire Dewitt and the City of the Dead*

"A gothic pastoral; a world of such beauty and menace that you scarcely recognize it as your own. Like Ambrose Bierce and Shirley Jackson, Hoffman has rediscovered America. Welcome home."
—Annia Ciezadlo, author of *Day of Honey*

"Hoffman's spare and delightfully strange stories are shot through with frequent flashes of sudden beauty. *RUIN* contains the seeds of her later award-winning fiction, along with her already fully formed voice. Each story in one way or another feels implicitly apocalyptic, in both senses of the word—the *end of the world* and *unveiling*."
—Panagiotis Kechagias, author of *Final Warning*

"Cara Hoffman's short fiction is as tense and rich with the opaque and the precise as a painting by Leonora Carrington."
—Molly Tanzer, author of *Vermilion* and *Creatures of Will and Temper*

"If there is such a thing as 'anarchist fiction,' it must be fiction that breaks all the rules of time and space, of realism and the fantastic, of fact and feelings. *RUIN* is true, exciting, anarchist fiction."
—Nick Mamatas, author of *The People's Republic of Everything* and *The Second Shooter*

"*RUIN*, like all the best story collections, is a glittering, abstract mosaic. From the uneasy fairy-tale rhythms of 'They' to the gritty, reality-shattering 'The Paragrapher' to the smooth, bitter drink that is 'Childhood,' each of these stories showcases a different aspect of Hoffman's razor-sharp talent—but they all demand that we confront hard truths and self-delusions. A treat for both fans of her novels and aficionados of the short story as an art form."
—Carrie Laben, author of *A Hawk in the Woods*

"In one of Schoenberg's compositions is the very evocative line 'I feel the wind of other planets.' Cara Hoffman's beautifully crafted stories bring that back to me. Tales of absence and possibility and other realms, rendered in unique voices. Haunting and excellent."
—John Zerzan, author of *Elements of Refusal*

Also by Cara Hoffman

RUIN

Cara Hoffman

RUIN
© Cara Hoffman
This edition © 2022 PM Press

ISBN: 978–1–62963–929–1 (paperback)
ISBN: 978–1–62963–931–4 (hardcover)
ISBN: 978–1–62963–930–7 (ebook)

Library of Congress Control Number: 2021945063

Cover Design by Matthew Lenning and Marc Lepson
Cover Art: "Inside this Little House," 1989 by David Wojnarowicz and Marion Scemama. Courtesy of the Estate of David Wojnarowicz and P.P.O.W.
Interior design by briandesign

10 9 8 7 6 5 4 3 2 1

PM Press
PO Box 23912
Oakland, CA 94623
www.pmpress.org

Printed in the USA.

For ML

The following stories were previously published in a different form: "DeChellis" in *Bennington Review*, "Waking" in *Our Stories*, "Childhood" in *The Opiate*, and "Retouch/Switch" in the anthology *Kink*, edited by Garth Greenwell.

CONTENTS

I never went to Troy; it was a phantom.
You mean it was only for a cloud that we struggled?
—Euripides, *Helen*

WAKING

After the boys had taken their flushed faces and the lingering spirits of their breath down the steps and back to the car, we would stay up and watch the black-and-white films we had made, projected against the gray cement of the basement wall. It was as if the night were only just now starting, at one or two in the morning, and we were suddenly entirely ourselves. The projector hummed and clacked. The focus was primitive, and we dealt with it by moving the entire apparatus forward or backwards on its folding chair. The outside shots were often overexposed. Sometimes we watched these films projected against a mirror that hung near the laundry room door. Sometimes against a sheet. Sometimes I would read a novel out loud while we went through every reel, over and over. *The Sheltering Sky. The Trial.* And all the while fields flashed by, birds flew, fires burned, bicycles raced past, eyes blinked and mouths smiled. Image after image made of light.

This would end around nine or ten in the morning and then we would go outside, sleepless and energized, to walk beside the stone-colored river. To walk along the trails. Sometimes we would shoot while we walked. Stills, super eight, Polaroids. Polaroids, she said, said everything. Their form alone, their very being. The subject of the photograph itself was irrelevant. It was how it came to be, she said. We filmed Polaroids as they developed. Oversaturated, grotesque, pulling their plastic genius into the silent light.

And we never talked about the boys, once they were gone. We

talked about the fastest way to get through school. You can, in tenth grade, graduate. You can. You don't even need perfect grades, just mediocre grades in upper-level courses. But what would we do then? What would we do then? I asked. She shook her head and smirked at me.

Stand over there, she said, pointing to a field of Queen Anne's Lace. Go into the middle of it. Kneel. Stand. Stand with your head turned. Take off your coat. Put it back on. Do that thing with your arms where they look like they spin all the way around in front of you. Good.

We didn't think to show them the films. We didn't film them. We didn't give them books to read. We didn't talk in the same tone of voice to them or when they were around. We said, Come over. Or we said, We'll meet you. We said, We'll be over later. We didn't care what they did. We didn't care where they were when they weren't with us. Disinterest sometimes made it necessary to terminate and replace. There was always another boy. Lying on the couch, sitting in the movie theater, or in the car. With the clothes they wore, with the seven-day stubble, with stereo equipment and various talents, or interests, gleaned from television. There was always another with his own "identity," immediate and plastic like a Polaroid.

I remember the silent lips parting and the gray smoke drifting out. I remember a shot, several seconds on the reel, of a girl skidding across the asphalt on her shin, grinning from the adrenaline before she took the skateboard up the halfpipe again. I can remember the shot of her lying in the grass laughing, her face wide and bright.

Run. And while you run, take off your clothes, till you are naked when you reach that tree, and then duck down in the grass to make it look like you were swallowed up by the earth. Good.

When the boys had taken their soft skin and their swollen mouths away, we would walk outside in the dark. We would walk through the empty neighborhoods shining beneath the street-lights. Until we reached the abandoned downtown. The parking lots beneath the constellations. The tall buildings cut out against the black sky. The cool air. The expanse of concrete. This is how we walked then. In an enormous loop that led back to the pools and gardens and fountains of the west side. And we swam behind our neighbor's houses, our quiet laughter drowned by the sounds of crickets. The smell of grass and chlorine, and our breasts were weightless in the water, like they weren't even there.

You can finish college at twenty. You can. You don't even need good grades. Just mediocre grades. You can finish at nineteen if you take twenty-four credits a semester. Then you're done. And you can go to graduate school then. You can finish grad school at twenty-two. You can have your PhD by twenty-three. You can. You simply can. You can have at least three or four books written by then. You can be working for the Associated Press. You can study at a conservatory. You can sell guns. You can work in an orphanage. Smuggle spice out of the East.

We would make it home in those last crepuscular hours and hunch over the sink gulping cold water from the tap. We would sleep side by side on the floor in long white V-neck T-shirts. Our eyes shut, reading an invisible page. Our eyelashes resting against the tops of our cheekbones. Our mouths open, sucking in the night.

We slept this way until we saw how the boys were coming into finer focus. They pressed their bodies against our jeans in hayfields behind the monastery at night, and we saw how they could be made beautiful. Inside the monastery basement, white candles burned for the dead, and outside in the fields the boys were ghostly images whose fascination lay in their unfolding and hardening form. But they were as yet interchangeable. Your fist closed around one the same as any another. And only one or two required further study, or became sentimental items in their familiarity. Became desired. And once desired, ruined our sleep. Ruined our sleepless wandering.

It was like this in East Berlin, she'd said about the boys. She'd been in Berlin for a summer studying art. The wall was still standing then and she'd written our names on it.

Wherever you went, she said, there was the same brand of coffee on the shelf. The same brand of aspirin. You couldn't get exactly the taste you wanted, but then you got used to what was there, and you liked it, no matter how crummy it was. No matter how weak. They're not Polaroids, she corrected me. They're like the coffee and the aspirin you buy in East Berlin. She said, you needed it to stay awake, or to not feel pain, and if it isn't working you just have more. They're like that.

Don't move, she said, in the grass outside the monastery. Don't move at all. It looks like you're a statue. It looks like you're a monument. You're a statue of the virgin skater. The great fallen tomboy.

We'll show them this film, she said. We'll have the coffee and the aspirin over for movies. I should shoot you from the back, she said, as I walk away. I should shoot this on nitrate film, so it will burn up if we leave it in the sun.

They sat in the dark basement and watched the films of the Polaroids developing, and the overexposed films, and the statue, and the girl swallowed by the earth. Their faces were bright. Reflections of images passed over them like shadows of clouds moving across the land.

After the reels were done and our eyes had adjusted, we didn't turn on the lights. We didn't ask them what they thought. We didn't offer them a drink. We didn't kiss. Or feel them. We just sat there in the dark.

That was a good night, she'd said about it. In retrospect, it seems you should have slept with one of them. It seems we should have done something other than rewind the reel. Maybe we should bring them on a walk next time. Maybe we should bring them swimming.

And then we slept on the couch in our clothes. Our long hair braided together on one side: blond, black, blond, black, blond. The tiny pale hairs on our cheeks nearly touching. And just before unconsciousness I could hear how her breathing was like her voice, how her throat held her voice and was full of sound and meaning, even as she quietly exhaled.

You can leave and never come back. You can stop speaking entirely and carry a little chalkboard with you on a rope around your neck, she laughed, because you can see how everything here is something other than what it is, can't you? Every blade of grass, every word, every inflection. Certainly, you can see that now, she said. You can see that silence is the whiteness of the sheet in the basement. And that we are waiting.

Waiting and waiting, we said in unison.

She said, right now it's as bright as heaven. It's as clear as night. The music of her voice carried as she spoke, like a little song, and I stopped walking to light my cigarette.

This whole beautiful world, she said, tears running down her face at last, as she grabbed the collar of my shirt, is a lie.

RUIN

The painting studio in Chinatown had a shower but no kitchen, five floors up, windows facing an airshaft, and it was either sweltering in there or dank steely cold; iced over panes by late fall, see your breath in winter. The ventilation was poor, and the smell of linseed oil and mineral spirits clung to my hair and I'd been working for ten hours straight when I decided to go out for a breath and a walk and ended up at the Salvation Army thrift store on 4th Avenue thinking I might find a lamp but instead watching a man who was holding an empty ten-gallon aquarium wander past jars of seashells and old rotary phones.

He wore a faded Black Sabbath T-shirt and had the occupied gaze of someone I would like to fuck or photograph; someone with a good body and concerns of his own who would go away without being asked.

His dark eyes reminded me of May; reminded me of the summer before I became poor and moved into my studio and May became rich and left the city.

We'd gone to Almayrac together and rented a house, in a lush pocket of nowhere near the Viaur River, with thatched roofs and tower ruins. Fields of lavender and yellow rapeseed flower surrounded the town. This was before the drought and before the fires; when the river wound through the hills and into the valley, pregnant and gleaming and lapping at the banks.

May had lain beside me in the courtyard while I drew, reading *The Lives of the Saints*; a catalog of sensational murders meant to inspire piety. The lives of the saints were all the same; cut short by arrows or fire or teeth or knives. Sun bled through the clouds and the heat rose thick and humid with new weather moving in; blackflies bit. Sweat ran into our hair and down our backs, and we decided to head into the cool of the valley, to the remains of the plague town.

Inside the Salvation Army it smelled like dust and mold and Lysol, and the man with May's dark eyes shifted the aquarium so he could look in his wallet, while the tall girls standing in front of him bought a pile of shirts with the name Strike Queens embroidered on the back. His presence was like a visual echo. A doppler image. He even stood like she did with his toes turned in, and the flush in his cheeks made the rest of his face look pale.

The sound of a siren rose and faded as traffic sped by on 4th Avenue and I didn't look away when he noticed me. His jeans were slung low revealing a hip bone, the curve of a tight belly. He had lovely hands.

On the way to the ruin, May and I had waded into the river, and out to a little island where mint grew tall and frogs crouched beneath the canopy of grasses, and we stood for a time in the pebbled shallows watching trout come to the surface to eat insects. After half an hour's walk the plague town emerged beyond a cornfield; amid a dark chunk of forest that rose from a depression in the earth. We walked down a deer path into the trees and beyond a fallen fortress wall, where it was ten degrees colder and the land was strewn with slabs of stone and moss-covered cobbles. In the center of the ruin a monastery listed like a boat at sea, its walls sunk deep into a muddy embankment populated by a colony of snails. Its arched windows framed a jungle of ferns growing tall inside.

Life was vivid with May; a swarm of butterflies rising from a field, a white horse with a black mane eating sugar from her hand, a warm humid wind bringing a cloud of termites.

The man with the aquarium paid and I watched his thick deft fingers slip the wallet back into his pocket.

C'mon, I said, when we got out on the street.

He said his name was James Day and that he'd grown up in Johnson City, New York, where it rained one hundred and ninety days a year. He told me the town was named after a shoe manufacturer and was known for its methadone clinic, its evangelical mega-church, and its designation as the Carousel Capital of the World. And it was there in Johnson City, he said, that he'd first thought of 'the solution'; in a warehouse with a corrugated metal roof, sitting on folding chair in an audience filled with the literal-minded, while his father raged into a microphone about the rewards awaiting them in the afterlife.

James Day was skilled and I was covered in his sweat and I wanted him gone, but his body; lean belly, wide wrists; his thick cock, pale purple, curving gently as he stood sated and growing soft.

But you can't prove nonexistence, I said. You can't prove god doesn't exist.

The glory of his chest, his hairless skin. I'd have to photograph him because if I let him stay to pose for a painting, he'd keep telling me things.

I have a PhD in neuropsychiatry, he said.

I put my shirt on.

Seriously, he said.

Uhuh.

I'm researching part of the brain hardwired for religious thought. That's why I was buying the aquarium.

Makes perfect sense, I said.

Really, he said. Think about it. Stories have a neurological basis, that's why they're consistent, right? There's only a certain number.

God or Jesus or Vishnu have one point of origin in the brain, and we know this because we can stimulate that part of the brain to produce consistent imagery. The divine and the journey to heaven is as common as the sensation of hunger.

Where do you live? I asked.

4th and D.

I handed him his underwear and told him I had to get back to work.

Where do you work?

I looked at him until he figured it out.

Here. Oh, here, of course. He turned his attention to the canvases. What are these about?

Excuse me?

The dog heads, he said. The naked men. The jellyfish.

That's what they're about, I said, then walked into the bathroom and shut the door. He kept talking while I washed him from my skin.

When I came out of the bathroom he asked if I wanted to see his frog.

Only if that's a euphemism.

I have mice too.

We all have mice.

Would you like to see them?

I bought a disposable camera on the corner of Essex and East Broadway because everything about his form begged reproduction. He talked while we made our way down Henry Street and then cut up Norfolk, past the abandoned Synagogue near the shaggy rat habitat of a parking lot by the Williamsburg Bridge. He talked while we crossed Delancey and Houston and up into the empty lots. We were mugged on Avenue B and he stopped talking only briefly to say, *Sure,*

sure, take it easy to a sweaty shivering boy holding a knife. The boy's face broke into a vision of relief as his fingers closed around two twenty-dollar bills.

A line of people waited outside a walk-up by the corner of 4th and D near the gut of a ruined tenement. His building was one door beyond that. The hallway smelled like piss and the floor sloped toward a cracked set of marble stairs where generations of hands had worn the banister dark and narrow. On the second floor, the words *living like a mouse* were tagged across a gray metal door and a trail of soot crept up the wall and across the ceiling. Another apartment had no door at all, just a tapestry hanging in its place. The third floor was damaged by fire, but the one above that was unscathed.

He pushed into the apartment and a musty antiseptic smell caught in the back of my throat, and he turned and locked the door shutting us into a tidy living room where steel grates covered the window. It was monastic, just a desk and a straight-backed wooden chair. There was a bathtub in the kitchen and a cage of mice and tanks full of stones and plants and a jar full of something red and oily and I thought this was a mistake.

James set the glass tank down next to a terrarium. When he reached under the sink, and began putting on a pair of latex gloves, I grabbed the back of his shirt and shoved him hard smashing his head into the counter, when he fell I stomped his back to keep him down, and went to kick him in the face but he was making a noise and there was fear in his eyes, and he wasn't fighting back.

What are you *doing*? Jesus Christ what are you doing? He said, Please. His hands up in front of his face now. That fucking hurt.

I thought—

I was going to show you the frog—why are you—you can't touch it with bare skin.

I fought the urge to take his picture when he spat blood into the sink. I said, It looked like—but there was no reason to finish the sentence. I might have pushed him because the apartment was too clean and quiet and smelled strange, and when he went for the gloves, I thought he would hurt me, or I might have pushed him because he hadn't shut up for nearly an hour.

Do I look like someone who could do something bad? He said, and he was curious, not trying to reassure me.

His cheeks were flushed, but his eyes were calm, and his skin was very white and smooth, and I didn't yet know why I was there; if it was loneliness, or if there was still something in his form and gesture worth stealing.

Of course you do, I said.

The frog was as big as the palm of my hand and the deep green of a forest at dusk. It closed its eyes slowly and I felt the weight of its muscles and the tenderness of its skin as it breathed.

James Day said if it weren't for the rubber gloves, I'd be in a coma.

Does it kill the mice?

It shuts down everything, drops their blood pressure, elevates their heart rates, causes paralysis; so you can make a good guess what parts of the brain are affected and how those correlate to a human brain, and we can determine and measure what chemicals are released in their bodies.

Does it kill them?

Not if the dose is right.

I set the frog back in its glass house and he threw the gloves into an orange container beneath the sink.

Bizarre, I said.

Says the hairless talking primate who shares DNA with a mushroom.

Why are you doing it *here*?

I don't have approval yet.

Columbia doesn't provide housing for professors?

Oh, sure they do. But—

He wasn't a junkie or a dealer but it was clear he needed to be there for a reason; near poor people, addicts, people who no one believed. Even if he was just some guy who wanted to extract neurotoxins from frogs and feed them to rodents to see what happened, he didn't need to do it there. I hadn't been wrong to knock him down.

James talked and I watched his body move as he set up the aquarium, filling the tank with moss and stones, and I thought of the glass exhibition cases at the museum of natural history, full of taxidermied animals labeled in Latin, given specimen numbers. Beside the display were cases holding reproductions of indigenous people who couldn't legally be taxidermied. Those were labeled with words like Peruvian Village and Seneca Nation. The vast cool rooms echoed with voices of children who'd been bussed there to see the stiff bodies of rabbits and foxes and monkeys, and to see the short brown mannequin wearing a wide-brimmed hat and holding a mannequin baby.

Shortly after we returned from Almayrac, May had fallen in love with a woman from California who photographed herself naked or dressed as characters from fairy tales and those display cases reminded me of the woman. How she captured her own face straining for praise as she attempted to look happy or thoughtful or brave; creating documents of self-obsession and neurotic despair, which she displayed as evidence of love and beauty.

And I remembered a child standing by the tank of mannequins

in Peruvian dress, she was holding a pink eraser shaped like a pig so that it could look into the display too.

He thinks they're real, she told me.

———————

I photographed him naked and holding the frog. And I photographed him dressed, extracting the neurotoxin from its skin.

Where did you grow up? he asked.

Where did you go to school?

How long have you lived in the city?

But I never thought about those things—or never thought of telling anyone those things. Especially not someone who was trying to make mice hallucinate so he could prove god didn't exist. He already knew what I looked like and how my weight felt pressed against him and how my skin tasted. Anything he'd missed was a failure of observation.

When my mother and I lived with Henry on 10th and B each of us had our own room on the second floor. My window overlooked Tompkins Square. Henry was recording a drone album and the vibration of it lived in the floor and in the walls and came up through my feet when I was painting. Sometimes we ate together at ten or eleven but mostly I ate peanut butter sandwiches and lettuce and at night we'd have studio visits. Hank would play what he'd been working on, my mother would read from her dissertation, and I would show them things I'd made with crayons or paint or chalk or dirt. I didn't tell James any of that. How my family, like his, believed in the divine.

He had a salvaged brass bedframe and the windows of his room overlooked a vacant lot, and all the light that would have been blocked by a five-story building poured in. Bookshelves lined the walls and I took his picture there too, in the light, and lay with him long past dark and into the morning, listening to the sounds of sirens and people coming and going on the stairs, and the high peeping song of the poison frog alone in its glass cage.

James Day was an ideal subject for painting. His shape and his gestures like a figure from a myth; like St. Francis the hermit communing with nature, like a monk in the monastery near Almayrac believing prayer and sacrifice would keep the plague outside the gates.

———————

Morning was a good time to leave his apartment. Someone was burning frankincense in the building to cover the bitter chemical smell of freebase, and a couple was fighting somewhere, one of them taunting: throw it down, throw it down, I fucking dare you. But none of it woke him.

Outside it was quiet and the sky was cloudless; a walk-up with a missing facade stood across the street, still half full of furniture, like a dollhouse missing a fourth wall, and the sidewalk was littered with glassine baggies stamped with a hand and a heart. Spaces where buildings had once stood opened up to the landscape and sky and made the remaining tenements seem solitary and vast. I passed a woman nodding out by a locked gate at the end of the block near the project towers; beyond her a visible sliver of the East River glinted gray in the sun. Alexandria, Beirut, Wiltshire, Delphi, Mayapan, a little slice of what's to come.

———————

Sammy Photo on Essex Street could process the film in an hour, so I waited by Seward Park where Chinese women were practicing military exercises to songs by Madonna.

Back at the studio the phone was ringing and the eight-foot

painting of a jellyfish was better after being away from it. I put the receiver to my ear and his voice came clipped and relieved.

You're alive, he said. What happened? You forget our studio visit?

I met a fella.

A fella like a girl with a crew cut and combat boots?

A fella like a man.

Are we using the word *man* to mean man?

How else would we use it?

Okay, listen, here's what you missed.

His phone hit something hard, then the static sound like a needle stuck in a groove; the low hum of droning feedback, double voices singing, bass and countertenor, a looped sample of me speaking and you could hear my lisp, so I set down the phone and went to brush my teeth, got in the shower and doused my body with peppermint soap. Watched paint swirl into the drain, got out, dried off, and put on a sari I'd bought at the Salvation Army, put my hair up in a rubber band. Then used a razor to scrape dried paint from the glass palate and squeezed the colors that would become James Day onto it.

Henry's song was still coming from the phone, but I could hear the bass drone getting stronger and knew it would end, so I picked up the receiver and put it to my ear for the last notes.

It's good, I said.

Yeah, it's good, he said. Stay put. Unka Hank's gonna bring over some breakfast.

Henry was a big, thick man, the size of a B-movie monster, with long salt and pepper hair and a nose that had been broken into a shape I'd loved since I was a child. He was dressed for work in black slacks and a white button-down with a frayed collar. And his stand-up bass was packed in the hard black plastic case strapped to his back and he carried it like it weighed nothing—set it in the only empty space near the sink. He handed me a coffee, then tore open the bag to make a picnic on the studio floor, where we sat cross-legged looking at the work and eating egg sandwiches.

What happened yesterday?

I handed him the pile of photographs and he went through them, tossing each back at me one by one.

Okay. You met a satyr . . . Who is the slave of a magic frog . . . The frog's a dope addict . . . You went to the pet store to see the mice . . . Then you visited the site of an earthquake. Fuck, where is this on D? You were over on D last night?

I held up the first photograph again, that gap of skin between his T-shirt and jeans. Gifted in bed, I said.

Looks it. He wiped his mouth daintily with a paper napkin and lit a cigarette. So what? The guy's doing a performance piece about captivity? What's he do?

He talks is what he does. Only time he was quiet was when his mouth was full.

He's an artist?

Said he's a professor.

Huh.

I set the brush down and stepped back. The gesture was right. It was James in weight and motion but it looked like me, the space between the eyes, the skin too dark. Even something in the frog looked like me.

Hank said, I don't think it's about a particular moment. And I didn't know what he was talking about, or if I had said something out loud that he was responding to. He said, You freeze time on the canvas and feel like you've got a superpower. But the paint is still eroding, the canvas is still decomposing, the real thing happens when you're making it, right? And this is like . . . shit. Like if someone was tracking you through the woods and they found it they'd know you'd been there.

If they found a painting I made, with my signature on it, they'd definitely know I'd been there, I said.

But that wasn't true of May's work. You had to dig to find her. Through pig intestine, shells, rope, slabs of marble and human hair, jumbles of melted army men suspended in shellac affixed to a boulder like moss; like she was rebuilding the natural world with presents brought to a witch's christening. The shape of the fern is the shape of the deer's tail, I thought, What natural camouflage do humans have other than lying?

You ready? he asked.

I zipped my boots back on.

Outside it was cool and bright, the first bites of fall and the distant breath of winter moved the leaves and it still smelled vaguely of sewer gas and ginseng, and the traffic on Allen Street coming off the bridge was too loud. At the East Broadway station, a couple sat together on milk crates reading different sections of the *Village Voice*, a cup of change at their feet. The man wore a shower curtain as a cape and the woman wore legwarmers and yellow work boots and a stretched-out one-piece bathing suit with a picture of the pyramids on it.

Artist or homeless? Henry asked.

I don't feel like playing.

Down in the cloisters of the subway we waited for someone to leave by the emergency exit and Henry ran for the door and held it open.

I'll remind you this not an act of thrift, he said. Guy my size could get tangled in that itty-bitty turnstile and they'd have to bring the jaws of life.

The train rushed in covered with graffiti and crowded except for one empty car, which no one on the platform entered, as if it were haunted. We pressed our bodies next to other people's bodies and we breathed their breath and smelled their cologne, and our skin was so close to their skin, so warm, and people stared at Henry for taking up space, his body an inconvenience.

Uptown was full of people whose great-grandparents made money they were still figuring out ways to spend. In the lobby at Lincoln Center Hank handed me the comp ticket and disappeared with his bass through a door marked private and I went out by the fountain to smoke. I'd been getting his comp tickets since I was eight, and had been smoking by the fountain since I was twelve, the same year he told my biology teacher I didn't have to dissect anything because we were philosophically opposed. Back then we were philosophically opposed to anything I didn't want to do.

––––––––––

At the diner after the show Hank said, I saw a notice up in the park. A guy looking for extras for a movie about hell. They're filming it by the Navy Yard. You go there and act like someone who would be in hell.

I've got the wrong hair for it, I said.

What are you talking about? You could get the part based on your hair alone.

Outside the sun was low over the Hudson, blinding orange through a corridor of towers. It was eighty blocks home, and the right weather for walking; we'd exhausted my job prospects in five minutes and the canvases would be dry by now, so I left.

Streetlamps flickered on as I passed through Chelsea, the city swelling with the sounds of evening; the smooth glide of traffic and horns blowing and the steady rise of voices overheard in passing talking all at once. Saying: *I imagine people sleep better having tiny proofs of the existence of the Eiffel tower . . . You can get it from swallowing, you can get it from a cut, you can get it from shit, you can get it from tears . . . She said she was a Marxist but when I took my coat at the end of the night she had all these shoes, she had hundreds of shoes . . . In the dream he was made of sugar and mercury and fur and I was sucking his dick on the floor of The Adonis . . .*

Below 14th Street I could smell smoke on the air from something vast and nearly extinguished. And I passed St. Marks and I thought of how much I loved images of St. Joan and how I would like to paint something that could stand up to them. Those statues of her armed, in full teenage glamour, that flanked the pulpits of little churches all along the Viaur.

St. Cecelia lived days beyond her failed beheading, bleeding from three deep cuts in her neck, and I thought of how I would like to paint her shape and the color of the wounds.

St. Francis died of malaria, with an eye infection that left him blind, sores on his hands and head. Death, he said, was the sister of God.

Hours later, alone on Division Street I turned on the bright lights, poured mineral spirits into an empty jar and put the needle in the groove. And I didn't care if I had money, and I didn't miss May, and I didn't see that everything in the city was about to be remade in the image of a mirror that reflects another mirror. And I went back in, giving weight to the flesh of James Day. Life beneath the line of muscle, life where there had only been color. Life to the black eyes, life to the palm that held the frog, life to the frog who was the sister of god.

THE APIARIST

The helicopter hovered above the girl, hovered above the still green retina of the in-ground pool, where the girl lay on her towel. A single, armed Adonis hung from the door, in his flak jacket, dark glasses, and boots, and she hoped it might land out on the long stretch of burnt prairie that rolled out to the perimeter fence. But it was caught as it descended, pulled up suddenly as if by an invisible wire, then banked just as fast, and was gone, over the yellow hill.

The air was thick with pollen and she lay sweltering beneath the scant shade of a battered awning by the abandoned cabana, reluctant to get up and cross the hot cement to slip beneath the murky water. She rested her arm over her face and began to drift, wishing she was back at work in that perfectly ordered world; the smell of wax and honey and wholesome fire; the little bellows puffing clouds of calming smoke into the hive so that she and Tetsuo could tend the bees.

A second helicopter passed lower this time, deafening, blotting out the sun, rippling the dry grass. She pulled the top of her bathing suit down exposing her breasts to the cool wind, and one of the soldiers leaned out to snap a picture. The first one was antipersonnel, this one was to document its work.

Above her, inaudible, the boy with the gun said, That was so *nice*.

Yeah, that's *all* Green's getting, said the boy with the camera.

That's all Green's ever got, said the boy behind the stick.

Green laughed. No, man, y'know f'real. It was just nice of her. It was the only living body they'd photographed that week.

Past the cinderblock dormitories and white plywood outbuilding and the long half-sunken bunker of the med-test lay the shade of the pomegranate grove where Tetsuo waited; zipped into his suit. She walked quickly, sweating, checking for gaps at her ankles and neck, making sure she was sealed in, running her gloved hands over the hood, looking for holes.

He raised a fistful of dead grass and she raised the green plastic lighter and flicked a spark by way of greeting.

Today they'd check the bees for mites, see if any had brought viruses home to the hive, exposed the queen. They'd scoop clumps of delicate bodies off the combs and examine the brood cells. See who was ready to be born, to learn the mapping flights, who had died and been re-absorbed. They'd mix oxalic acid with sugar and spray it on frames. And they would stand together as they did each day, silent at the center of the circumambient hum, unable to see each other's faces, their voices muffled or spent from heat and thirst and fatigue.

Tetsuo Uber was the great-great-grandson of the inventor of the hanging frame. The file cabinet–like constructions where bees build their hives; white boxes that could be seen in other places, stacked in lone meadows or by the crests of highways, somewhere near fall flowers, near berry bushes or orchards.

Outside the apiary's little grove there was nowhere else to go, besides the swimming pool and the dust road that ran along the perimeter fence. She took the job because she could work in the field instead of the lab; be outside, be visible from the air in case some kind soldier flying over had room for a passenger. If there was any dying to do it wouldn't be done underground, or in a crowd, the thought of dying in a crowd was unbearable. And these details factored into the dysteleology that she somehow considered to be decisions she'd made—a kind of self-determination brought about by fate; brought about by narrowing the concentric circles of providence.

They worked without speaking, baking in their white suits, and it was only in the packaging plant or the changing room where they wiped sweat from their faces and smoked and shuffled over to drink from the fountain that she could see him; pale like a creature who lived near the ocean floor, his face deeply lined, arms dotted with the raised scabs of stings, dark intelligent eyes. She handed him the shipping forms for a case of propolis and he signed his name beneath hers, the percussive scrape of the pen like a match being struck.

Her signature never appeared alone, was always followed by detainee number and housing bloc number, the same numbers which were stamped inside her boots, and on the collar of her protective suit. Still, a signature is all it takes to get you work in zones of disaccord; places that no longer mattered or may soon become unmapped. And she'd determined that this work would be instructive down to the cellular level; would rebuild (through the resistance to stings and the consumption of honey) whatever discipline or determination it was that floated the helicopter day trips of armed beauties with telephoto lenses. That kept them weaving a rope of sand, kept them hovering between corpses and the exposed breasts of women in work camps.

When it was clear that she had studied somewhere, they asked if she knew anything about entomology. Having just come from six weeks in an experimental trial in the med-test, and still seeing halos around each tree, faces rising from the dirt, spiders shimmering in every drop of water, she told them yes, yes.

The sheets smelled like sweat and smoke and the room was hot, but the house was her own; a particle board cube with a tarpaper roof and cracked solar panels near an outcropping of limestone by the billets. Such freedom. At night the big cats shrieked like wind, the stars were no different than before. Dreams were still landscapes of sex and food and cities, keys that worked, locks that broke, a getaway car, the ability to swim in the sky. Or dreams were of Tetsuo lying beside her, his belly rising and falling, his breath making no sound while she drew on his skin with the tip of a finger; signing her name, writing about the algae thick as moss on the swimming pool walls; about the pieces of waxy comb she chewed to keep from feeling hungry. No touch could wake him, in the dream, no story. The curtainless windows in the dream are black. A single lethargic bee crawled in the corner of the sill, and it turned out it could speak. And then there was the siren and she ran to put her boots on, to head for the border fence, but it's only the siren that signals the start of day.

She picked up a pound of margarine, a pound of rice, two loaves of white bread, coffee, apples, a pomegranate, two packs of cigarettes; more than enough food to supplement the meat kit. She ate honey by the tablespoon. She went to the billets when she was sure she wouldn't see another human face, especially the short timers, or the people who'd just arrived. They didn't pretend they were somewhere else—like home—like an apartment or a hotel or a college internship. They didn't pretend they were an apprentice to an artisan, or a scientist. They didn't go to the pool, though they could. No one went to the pool but the girl. The other prisoners were housed two or five to a barracks. Most of their work was in the factories, and some were employed, what could be called employed, in the medical-testing facilities.

Tetsuo had a bicycle, and a ring of keys, a cat, an account at a bank, and a garden of grasses and stones, but he was still inside the fence, serving his sentence too, from inside a green shingled house on a rise to the east of the apiary. When the helicopters ceased to pass, Tetsuo would not be traded for another living body, nor for a dead body, nor pieces of a dead body, nor for information. When the helicopters ceased to pass no one would show up to debrief him. He would put on his yellow helmet, put his cat in a side pouch, and ride his bicycle away.

Or when the helicopters ceased to pass nothing would happen. No one would be traded, or debriefed. No one would go home and there would be silence, there would be winter. The girl and Tetsuo would produce honey for no one to pick up. The women in the med-test and the women in the factory would wander away, not worth a bullet. The difference between authority and the lack of it having had, after all, no real distinction. Several years investment in the outskirts of inhumanity would have been dissolved by the day-to-day, by common language, by the undeniable likenesses in form, and all that form disguises. People—even the girl—could remember that California wasn't always like this. Or maybe, she thinks, they could remember that it was always something like this. Believing in a future, any future, was a luxury she had because of Tetsuo. Her skin wasn't a petri dish for variations on entropy, or the thin red landscape for chemical burns, observed with a lover's steady mastery of the detail. She was not looking into human eyes that looked into her human eyes, while feeding her chemicals that had yet to be named. Neither was she sitting with her mind in blank repose as she helped build some or other mysterious item for deployment.

She kept bees. She swam between the tile crosses at the ends of the algae-covered lap lanes, and this was not the apocalypse of her dreams. This was no uncovering. No peeling back the surface to reveal anew, Adam and Eve amid the rubble, back-to-back, a four-legged creature that could at last think and do on its own. And she thought about Tetsuo's veined white hands as he suited up, and later as he lit his cigarette—the languidness there, a defeat or inertia, or simply biding, waiting.

———————

For three thousand years people had been eating honey that had first passed through thousands of tiny mouths; made from particles of yellow dust, that hung in the air and coated the stamens of flowers, honey that was made in a home constructed of nectar and spit. And there was poison too, she remembered; a story about a hive near a mechanic shop, bees drinking antifreeze, making green honey. And ancient poison too; the honey from the rhododendron flower, she thought, which wiped out a Roman invasion near the Black Sea, soldiers poisoned, helpless.

She drew new houses for the bees with a stub of a pencil that had been left in her room, schematics that would increase the production of the Apis Meliflora, and gave them to Tetsuo before they opened the hive.

Why do you think they'll produce more inside this construction? he said.

It expands the space for brood cells, she said, without having to stack another super.

It would require more fertilization to produce more females. This doesn't simplify anything. You can assume the hive will self-regulate, especially Meliflora, but you can't predict the initial response.

It's compensated for after the new brood matures.

The Uber design has remained unchanged for one hundred and eighty years because it works.

But they'll use any space, said the girl.

No, he said. Sometimes they leave. All of them.

He tossed the drawing to the ground and pumped the bellows and the smell of burning grass and paper filled the air. She lifted the lid of the white box and slid a frame out, and the bees moved toward their food, murmuring, gorging.

Every day was not the same, even for the bees. Even though their world burned down, and then ceased to burn down, with great regularity.

If the world was on fire, the girl said, watching their yellow bodies move like one trembling creature through the smoke, it wouldn't make me hungry. It wouldn't make me work.

Tetsuo looked up at her, Oh, no? he said.

The next afternoon seven helicopters passed over the pool as she swam. A cloud of them. A swarm, a flock, like with crows—is it a murder? A murder of helicopters passing. The stuttering chop and whump of blades reverberated through the landscape and they were not on voyeur maneuvers, they were not low enough to cause a breeze or moving slowly enough for her to catch a glimpse of who was inside.

The smell of burning rubber caught in her throat each time she broke the surface to take a breath. The pool was warm as bathwater and she swam close to the bottom, opening her eyes to the hazy green that covered the walls like moss, the black crosses that marked the end of each lap lane were barely visible beneath. She reached out to touch one but jerked her hand away revulsed, shuddering at the slickness.

What was the state of the Pacific? How was it to swim there now? Last time she had seen the ocean was at night and the black water lapped at the coast. All she wanted was the rising world of water dark and deep. No heat, no hum, no baking dust, no songs of artillery.

In the beginning, when she first came to the camp, she believed a passing helicopter was bound to drop down long enough to pick her up, to set her somewhere outside the fence. She could walk from there to safety. Or could have if it weren't for the mines, if it weren't for the food she'd miss. If it weren't for Tetsuo's closely shorn hair or the way he hardly needed to shave, or the way he held his hands when administering drugs to insects, his hands nearly weightless holding their fragile bodies. It was not the pale skin at his wrist, she thought. No one is imprisoned by the blue veins beneath the pale skin at someone's wrist. If you've been saved from hunger and fire, if you swim and walk and speak, while others burn, are you still a prisoner?

She swam until exhaustion, then lay in the sun watching a dark column of smoke billowing up from the earth beyond the hillside thinking of the fisherman and his soul. She'd read about him back when the library was still standing.

The fisherman had fallen in love with someone who wasn't human, so he stood by the sea and cut his soul away at the feet; not to repent but so that he could live with her. When he was free from his soul, he dove into the ocean to join his love, to become her comrade.

Every year his soul would come to the shore and beg for him to return; bribe him with the riches of experience; stories of beauty it had seen, how it had lain in the snow beneath the northern lights, run beside the strongest animals, listened to the voices of children ringing like bells. It had watched the sun shining low and orange through a corridor of glass towers; had danced and wandered, cooked and eaten, slept and woken. It had watched the stars fill the black night. But these stories meant nothing to the fisherman and each year he refused his soul.

After many years of these stories, the soul came around torn and filthy, pleading, telling the fisherman of his thefts, and cruelties, and finally murders. And fisherman listened no more, leaving the soul wandering, howling in rage and grief at the water's edge. How could it have done anything but beg and plead and kill without its heart? This, she thought, was the apocalypse of man. All soul. Opportunistic soul, starving soul. Gorged on blood until there is no more, then weeping to its own form for reconciliation. Pleading for the return of a thing that will make it do right.

Once, stung inside her ear, the mean spike brought such immediate rage she screamed, toppled the hive. Tore her hood off and stomped it. Her jaw was throbbing, her eyes were burning, streaming; the tiny dart was still in her ear—a needle with an abdomen connected to it. Bees landed on her skin and Tetsuo dropped the smoker at her feet, held her shoulders with gloved hands, he said, Stay inside your body. When that happens, you stay inside your body.

She'd always had luck: a corner of the public library instead of a bed; blinding white light that swallowed the street where she'd lived, no money to secure a trip farther than the edge of the ruined town. Without that kind of luck, she'd be dead now. Wouldn't have been picked up at all. Wouldn't have had a free trip to a tech colony. Without luck like that, she might be rising in a column of oily ash.

———————

She mentioned the helicopters as they sat on the benches in the packaging plant and he didn't respond; unzipped his suit and lit a cigarette. She'd seen him every day for two years, and in most of that time he had worn the white suit. In all of that time they had spoken about insects.

When he pulled off his boots and placed his bare feet on the tile she could feel the coldness of the floor in her own body.

I'll come with you to the pool, he said.

She walked over to drink from the fountain.

Tomorrow, he said. After we look at the Meliflora.

That night she dreamt she was down with the fisherman, in a cathedral of sound, in the black Pacific. The water was thick with voices whose harmonies shifted in weight and density. And that sound was glorious and everywhere, pressing against her eyes, pouring into her mouth, pulling her flesh.

The fisherman showed her his home with such pride; but it was as green and empty as the pool and she saw now that his teeth were shells, a weed flapping raggedly between them. He swam with his love and she was white and hideous like a thing that's never come to the surface. And no one had ever looked as happy as the fisherman; down there all body and heart. But the song that flowed through them, that lifted them like waves, it wasn't a choir at all. Whose song is this? she asked but knows already that it was his soul. Beneath the sky's dark mirror, inside the sea's heavy belly his soul's misery had become his heart's delight; the music they lived by, the walls of their home.

The girl was waiting for Tetsuo in the heat, her feet hanging over the side of the pool. The smell of algae and smoke thick in the air.

He walked, wearing gray shorts and rubber sandals, barechested, a diving mask pushed up on his forehead, another in his hand. She'd never seen so much of his body before.

And she looked down at her arms, dark, burnt, peeling. Her hair was black and dull from sun and chlorine and dust. A gunmetal, washed-out black. And she looked away as he got closer, fighting the embarrassment at not seeing him in his protective suit, and of feeling herself a piece of kindling.

We received a new shipment of Apis Dorsata, he said, handing her the other mask, and squatting before her on the concrete, elbows resting on his knees.

The rubber straps felt stiff and crumbly as she slid it over her head.

No one raises Dorsata, she said. They're like dinosaurs.

We do now.

You can put them by the pomegranates, she said. But it's hard to imagine they'll be happy enough to stay, and those stings.

They won't need the trees, he said, we'll be feeding them ourselves.

She thought, Nothing has changed in three thousand years.

I won't make poison, she said

You won't be making it, he said. But it's interesting, don't you think? Even that it's possible. Something new to study.

She thought, It's the smallest details that form the autonomy in every slavery, the slavery in each choice that's made. The compulsion and the reflex, the opposing symmetries. Eighty thousand bees in the hive hear, with the hairs on their legs, a song that tells them where to find food. Each bee sings with its body, its own song of proximity. And every woman at the med-test walks there on her own. Because they have all, she understood now, looking at Tetsuo's scarred and solid chest, left the body. Like the miserable murdering soul, they'd been pulled from the body; like the bee left its soft stomach and spike in her ear. And maybe all of them were languishing like that bee, unnoticed, dying, dismembered. Their last involuntary reflex having pulled them inside out.

He slipped off his sandals and put his feet in the water, slid his lean body in, and strapped the goggles over his eyes, and they swam in their separate lanes, to the crosses at the end.

With the mask everything was clear; the water full of particulate life shining gray and silver and green. Sunlight illuminated the cement floor; a web of cracks eclipsed briefly by a helicopter passing above. The algae covered walls were bright and Tetsuo swam beside her, and she saw the architecture of his legs, of his back as he crested to breathe, as he moved through the veil of green, through the bands of gold light, close enough for her to touch.

After many laps she didn't look at him, and then he was gone, standing in the shallow end, barely visible a glitch of movement amid static. She dived to skim the bottom and stand beside him.

It was refreshing, he said, and pulled himself up, standing on the hot cement, running a hand through his hair. You can keep the mask, he said, then turned, walked away barefoot, sandals dangling from his fingers.

The girl moved into his lane and kept swimming, and as she neared the wall she saw shapes cut into the algae like a petroglyph.

In the slick green life, at the center of the cross, he had written her name with his fingertip. And she read it, weightless in the green and luminous pool, while above the quiet swarm of spinning blades cut the light in two.

CHILDHOOD

It was my childhood dream to become either an alcoholic or a very old man. After thinking it over it became obvious that the latter, though it would be more difficult to achieve in the short term, would afford me more respect.

I dressed in brown corduroy pants and oxford shirts, tweed sports jackets and loafers. I kept a pack of Players navy-cut cigarettes in my breast pocket and read Ibsen. I went out regularly by myself to cafés and to plays put on at the college, for which I only had to pay a child's admission price. I bought a pair of leather slippers and a smoking jacket. Every evening I would sit in front of the television watching *Sixty Minutes* and drinking ice water mixed with vanilla from a scotch glass. It was a quiet life. I was thin and long-limbed and easily mistaken for a boy. I am certain that some days, while waiting for the bus, if the light was right or if my back was turned, people thought I was indeed a little old man.

I began wearing a tweed cap. I had six or seven ties given me by my father, and had purchased another four from the Salvation Army. I had more and better-quality neckties than any girl my age. I was also able to find a pocket watch at Goodwill for fifty cents.

Once my wardrobe was established, I began to listen to swing music. And it was then I realized that I had been a music critic before my retirement. I missed my apartment in the city, and my desk in the newsroom where I had sat composing my columns, cigarette smoke catching in the orange light that came through the metal blinds. I missed my rapport with the musicians and my free tickets to their performances. I missed the other writers, and I especially missed Diego Rivera and his wife, whom I'd met briefly when Diego was painting a mural at Rockefeller Center. I began to wish I'd never agreed to move in with my daughter and her husband, the psychologist. I did not like the countryside and couldn't stand my daughter's taste in decorating, which struck me as somehow both bucolic and pretentious. But mostly I hated that my daughter referred to me as "Toots," and insisted I attend dance lessons every day except weekends. The lessons were humiliating. My class was composed of a group of scrawny girls with missing teeth who dressed in pink tights and white leotards. Often, I was singled out in class and placed at a small bar in the middle of the room, so these children could observe my technique. Which was, I'll admit, precise. But it was also uninspired. When my daughter picked me up from dance lessons she would say, How was class, Toots?

I need to find some peers, I would tell her, thinking of Rivera and Kahlo, and my friend Man Ray. This can't go on. I raised you better than this.

She said, I found a chain for your pocket watch.

I took to reading all day, listening to swing music on my son-in-law's stereo with a pair of gray plastic headphones. My son-in-law, the psychologist, oddly referred to me as Beauty, but then they say that only the disturbed make good psychologists. He would come home in the evening and say, How's my little Beauty? And I would peer at him from over the paper and rattle the ice in my glass. I couldn't imagine how my daughter had married such a man. They were both a disappointment.

Finally, I told my daughter flat out I could no longer attend Madame Helena's School of Dance.

She was trained in the Soviet Union, my daughter said, hoping to appeal to the party politics of the era in which I once wrote.

I don't care, I told her. It's humiliating. I can't wear that ridiculous costume anymore.

But look what you wear every *day*, Toots. You look so cute in your leotards. You look so free, like a little girl should.

I shook my head; the very idea.

Listen, I said, I appreciate you paying for the lessons. I realize you and your husband are only trying to make my stay here less boring. But this isn't the way. I used to take in a lot of ball games at the Polo Grounds, maybe there's some athletic program going on over at the senior center.

You're staying in dance, she said. You've been in dance since you were a little peanut. We're not throwing away nine years of study.

I wouldn't exactly call it study. Maybe I could pick up some freelance work for the local paper, I told her, and she began to cry.

I'm sorry, I said. I can no longer cram my tired old feet into those leather and wooden torture shoes. I rattled the ice in my vanilla water nonchalantly, to show her who was the parent. I produced an excellent smokers cough, then took a handkerchief from of the pocket of my dressing gown and wiped my forehead. I'm just too tired, I said.

When my son-in-law came home he said, Hey, Beauty Rose, Mom said you're quitting dance.

Who? I asked him, not even bothering to set the paper down.

What's going to happen to Daddy's little ballerina? he asked.

I cleared my throat and ignored him.

I remained silent instead of giving him the comeuppance he deserved for speaking to me that way. And because he did provide me with bus fair and spending money. But his remark convinced me that he was sexist. As a member of the Socialist Labor Party, I believed there should be a continual exchange of mutual, temporary, and above all voluntary authority and subordination. The more I thought about it, the more I realized this sexist authoritarian had warped my not-so-bright daughter's understanding of the world. I couldn't believe she was foolish enough to anchor her identity to a man who would use the phrase *Daddy's little ballerina*.

They dropped the topic of dance and I went about my daily activities, reading and taking in plays, watching the news and drinking my vanilla water. I resigned myself to living with them. I tried out different caps. I thought my only annoyance now would be my daughter's habit of cutting my sandwiches into little hearts. This I tolerated because I had never liked crust.

With dance lessons safely in my past I had more time to read and to practice what I felt to be one of life's great joys, jumping rope. A man my age needed a certain amount of cardiovascular exercise, and since I'd been a featherweight boxer in college, I had gotten used to jumping rope as part of my training. Every afternoon I would jump rope for an hour or so in my daughter's driveway. I found that singing helped pass the time while jumping so I sang some of those great American traditional songs like "Engine Engine Number Nine" and "Miss Lucy Had a Steamboat." We used to sing those songs around the office to determine who got stuck with the dull assignments. No one wanted to be O-U-T. This practice gave me a great deal of pleasure, except when it was interrupted by my daughter bringing one of her heart-shaped sandwiches down the driveway and setting it off to the side with a glass of ice tea. She usually said something insipid like, You look so cute, Toots, or All that jumping must be getting you hungry, Tootsie pie.

I also had a great deal of time to observe the interactions between my daughter and her husband. It seemed that my daughter spent her days vacuuming, doing laundry, cooking, watering plants, and rearranging furniture. Her husband would come home every evening and fall asleep on the couch, after an exhausting day of siphoning off the dysfunction of others in the community. When he awoke, he would recount this dysfunction through a series of vagaries and platitudes that appeared to represent professionalism. He was like an employee of a uranium mine, coming home after digging and making his family radioactive. In reality his demeanor expressed an ego that had long gone unchecked, a martyr complex, a chauvinism, poorly developed intellectualism, and misanthropy so thinly veiled I was certain he had chosen his career to exact some sense of power over his own neurosis and emptiness. Every day when he came home and they kissed in the doorway, it was *Cinderella* meets *The Emperor's New Clothes.* Cinderella whistling while she wove a mantle of false confidence for him through her own ambitionless materialism.

Hey Beauty Rose, my son-in-law would say to me. Who is Daddy's little girl? I would stare blankly at him and he would laugh and shake his head. You're always going to be Daddy's little girl no matter how big you get, you know that, don't you? Sometimes he would stand by my daughter as she worked in the kitchen, with his arms folded across his chest and say things like, That's not the way you make vegetable stock, *is* it? or, pointing to something just below his fingertip, You better wipe that up.

Then he would sit at the table and drum his fingers in different arhythmic patterns while she worked. The finger drumming sometimes led to whistling, so that all of the work being done, or in my case the reading being done, moved to a kind of counter-musical human noise, a nagging of taps and shrills that seemed meant somehow to suck all internal attention, all thought or personal contemplative pleasure, toward the rattling that radiated out from his position at the table. As a person whose musical sensibility was finely tuned, I found this unbearable.

My son-in-law's need for attention put everyone around him in a constant state of interruption. My daughter did nothing about this, though I observed her annoyance. Finally, one evening I looked up from my book and asked him to stop this practice. He laughed and beamed into my face with great condescending affection, What? Don't you like Daddy's whistling? My request seemed to bring out a great need for him to continue this behavior whenever he was home. As if it were a game we now had. Being asked to stop amused him a great deal. If you turned and tried to engage him in a productive manner, to dissuade his fidgeting he would lecture you on his favorite topic: child abuse. He would detail graphic accounts of child abuse going on nearby, but by whom he couldn't disclose. These impassioned speeches to us were a great complement to the noise in terms of intrusiveness. If you began to tell him about your day, his eyes would glaze over. He liked to lecture with a melancholic nostalgia about himself. As if he were, in fact, some poltergeist of a man that had once had enough self-possession to just be quiet.

My own daughter was not much better, but to her credit, I believe she had been driven insane through constant interruption and disrespect. Whenever she looked as if she were about to say something about his behavior, he would tell her she was beautiful. This had a terrifically pacifying effect on her. Almost as if she had been drugged. It seemed to me she had been much brighter as a child. The only minor consolation was that, despite what they thought, they had no children of their own.

Eventually the fact that I had nowhere else to go began to wear on me. I gave up attempting to read or ponder anything of significance when they were around for fear of interruption and the negative feelings associated with it. I could achieve nothing now that I had moved in with them; I could feel my mind and heart beginning to atrophy and my independence and self-esteem suffered terribly. They were poor conversationalists, with little understanding of politics and no genuine appreciation for beauty. I could not show them the writing that I or my friends had done, or play them the recordings of the music I loved. I feared that doing such things would result either in my son-in-law bastardizing the work through amusical mimicry, or my daughter buying me a nightshirt with a picture of Cab Calloway on it.

My financial dependence on them made me feel like some kind of scab. I hadn't felt so low since the Triangle Shirtwaist fire, when all those little girls were burned to death because the owner of the factory barred the doors shut. I longed to be put in a nursing home.

A nursing home? My daughter asked incredulously. You're eleven years old, she laughed and tugged at the brim of my cap.

Each day I would consult my pocket watch to make sure it was after twelve p.m. before I began to drink. As a newspaper man, and former featherweight boxer, I was familiar with intoxication. Not sloppy intoxication, but the kind required to get through the type of situation I currently found myself in. A tight-lipped kind of intoxication that makes dealing with bores and anti-intellectuals either tolerable or amusing. The kind that draws you out into the big picture, so far out that you can take comfort in the idea of the sun exploding, and then everything seems so temporary and insignificant.

I would wake up, spend several hours reading, practice my rope-jumping regimen, listen to the BBC World Service on the radio, then pour myself two shots of Grand Marnier from a large bottle I had found in the pantry. Later in the day I might have another. I also took up napping.

Meanwhile, my daughter appeared to have finally snapped. She spent more and more time in front of the mirror applying various treatments to her face. Curling her eyelashes, sucking in her cheeks, and repeating certain phrases to her reflection. She tried out different expressions. One in which she would raise an eyebrow and turn her head slightly to the left, while still meeting her own gaze, was particularly disturbing. For a while this benefited me, as she left me alone. She stopped making my sandwiches and doing my laundry. It seemed that when she was speaking to me, she was trying out different voice modulations, laughs, and body postures that were meant for some invisible person. She was unable to look at me without her strange new rehearsed face. Or the distracted look of calculating what that face's affect would be on the invisible person. Between her husband's noise and her posturing to the unseen, the house felt very crowded.

She began to read cultural-theory books, which I took as a positive sign, until I realized that they were being used as props, and also scripts. The language in the books was used in the same way the glance in the mirror was. Only in this case, I was the mirror. In an affected voice, slightly lower than her own, with a tone of gravity and suggested world-weariness she would parrot Gloria Steinem, while dressed in a sheer silk blouse purchased with her husband's credit card. Steinem as coquetry. I thought briefly that it might be some kind of performance art, and that my daughter was actually a genius. But that was parental blindness, a hope that I hadn't failed completely.

I suggested she read some Emma Goldman and she gave me a practiced smirk, as if she knew who that was. While I couldn't fault her for realizing that women had it bad, I had no idea how she meant to make her life, or any woman's life, better by this new behavior.

I went back to reading the paper and drinking my Grand Marnier on the rocks. I had begun to time it so that I would be just intoxicated enough to tolerate my son-in-law's yammering when he arrived home. My daughter now responded to being called beautiful by acting as though she had been slapped. The loathing she had adopted for my son-in-law seemed completely out of proportion to anything he had actually done. And it was amazing, and also hilarious to watch, particularly after a few drinks. It was as if they were reading from a script of a Soviet propaganda play meant to instruct on the corrosive, soul-crushing, and intellect-warping evils of capitalist society.

It wasn't long before my son-in-law stopped talking to me altogether. I guess it was because I had raised his wife, and admittedly done such a poor job. But the finger tapping continued and was now coupled with an aggressive and sarcastic grimace in my direction. My daughter was not home often and no longer cooked meals for us. My son-in-law would eat on the way home from work. I would make myself spaghetti with butter and drink vanilla water or whatever wine was in the house. I still took in plays. I did my own laundry, my own shopping. I watched *Sixty Minutes*. I read. I jumped rope.

And I remembered the days when I was a writer, the orange light slanting through the metal blinds in the newsroom, singing "Engine Engine Number Nine" with the other staffers and going out to listen to jazz. I remembered how strong the women were, and how genuine the men. I remembered those little girls in the Triangle Shirtwaist Factory. And how we all cried down at the pub after work the day they burned to death.

THE PARAGRAPHER

From a distance she can see the crew gathered; yellow tape strung from tree to tree and men with radios at the periphery. The snowflakes are large and coming down fast, settling thick on the black branches surrounding the site, drawing all sound nearer, up into itself. Her boots don't crack the surface rigor mortis of yesterday's snowfall; one hundred pounds, she's held aloft on it, and even at her hasty gait, her footprints disappear behind her.

Lights have been set up. The pile of dirt beside the dig is already covered in white. White everywhere. There are men with shovels and men with radios, an ambulance driver, channels 7 and 15, standing by, suited and lipsticked; and in the dimming light, silent and slight, among the depredators and fingersmiths, Flynn.

———————

Flynn taps the replay on the transcriber, and the voice of White's best friend slides through the headphones and into her ears. This has been going on for close to a year. Her foot hits the transcriber, and then voices push into her head. Her fingers strike keys concordant with the sounds, and her eyes stare at the screen, reflecting each word as it forms, on a glassy sheen covering a web of broken blood vessels.

In this way she closes a circuit around Wendy White's life. The who, what, when, where of it. The accumulation of details. The testimonies and vacuities that lead where they always do. Flynn has listened to the sentences so many times she can account for every pause, every raised intonation, every uh or cough that the tape repeats.

———

—the cops. And then we filed all the paperwork, like, on that Tuesday and it was fuckin'—can I say—
ke, on that Tuesday and it was fuckin'—can I say fu—
and it was fuckin'—can I say fuck? You won't put that in right?
put that in right? Anyway, just a sec . . . okay, so by Friday we were like—
—y Friday we were like, man! Something fucked up has happened, y'know? And we were like, aren't they gonna look for her? 'Cause—
pened, y'know? And we were like, aren't they gonna look for her? 'Cause—
onna look for her? 'Cause sh—

———

Flynn is in the back seat looking out. She can see the girl's breath dissipating as it rises toward the streetlight near the driveway on Lisbon Avenue. She watches the white vapor for a while before realizing it's coming from Sarah's mouth, from her lungs, up through her body to converge with the light pollution and factory blowover. Sarah is standing beside the Chevy, peering into glass gone reflective in the dark. She's has to get closer to see. Her breath steams up the window and she rubs it clear with a Thinsulate mitten, presses her forehead to the pane and curves her hands to block out the glare. Seeing Flynn, she raises her eyebrows and smiles involuntarily, then looks shocked, turns and runs back up the driveway.

The storm door snaps shut and there's hollow stamping of boots on the carpet, audio from the loud TV, a chorus of sylphadine voices singing about razor blades.

She's still crying, Dad, the girl calls out and Flynn can see it in her head like she's floating above the living room. One of Sarah's socks is inside out and she pulls at the ridged end of its seam, leaning against the door frame.

Okay now. Leave. Her. Alone. Sarah, I *told* you—

The snug seal of the door, a muffled squeak, then quiet.

Snow blows sideways in the light of the lamp and four or five boys pass, walking in the middle of the road where it's plowed. Flynn watches them as if she's at the drive-in, like their forms are projected on rain-damaged rippling fabric in the distance.

She doesn't know how many hours she's been sitting in the car, because it's been dark all the while. The city lights have done little to obscure the stars, and she has watched them slip up beyond the tops of the windows. The Chevy's back seat is bigger than the couch in her apartment, she can easily lie down. Her face is sticky, is alternately warm and freezing. Her red hair is plastered to her cheeks, it's wet inside her ears. She's holding a pencil tight in her fist.

No one's shown up for a while to look at her, and she's happy that no one has asked again if she'd like to go somewhere or come in and warm up. It's actually not bad with the blanket and her body heat in the confined space. The cold is good and bracing and she continues to cry; resigned to it, second nature now. She can laugh while doing it, carry on a conversation, anything. Yesterday, before she got her big break, these kind of powers wouldn't have seemed possible.

———

Down in the cold by the loading dock, the air smelled like ink and soot and the sweet odor of cornflakes coming from the stacks of the Kellogg's plant, and she stood smoking with Liberatore, passing the cigarette back and forth, while big men in Carhartts tossed neat cubes of bundled newspapers onto a truck.

When Joe came out, he was holding her notebook and she could tell by the look on his face but waited for him to say it.

You were right, girl. It's that site by the reservation.

And she whispered yes, tossed the cigarette. High fives all around.

Joe said get going. But she'd already grabbed the notebook from his hands, hopped down to the wet pavement, and was running to her car. Four pens in her coat pocket, another impaling a knot of hair at the back of her neck.

Pick up a carton of Marlboros, Liberatore called after her. They're tax-free on the res.

The fear of getting there at all makes her sprint, hard little flecks of ice hit her face with the sting of iron filings, and she's already got the questions lined up in her head, she's already thinking in third person, seeing it from above, planning the lede, seeing her byline on one.

———————

r her? 'Cause she's been gone for a week and all her stuff is—
for a week and all her stuff is at the apartment and her b—
artment and her boyfriend is freaking out, like ready to fu—

———————

Now Flynn is turning to dust in the back seat of a big American car. Traveling in time, back beyond the missing Wendy White. Beyond Wendy White's disappearance and her still only-imagined murder. Back before Flynn had made her name on the hair and sperm on the couch and the blood on the floor. Before she considered how the vowels should ring, how the syllables should syncopate in a sentence about a cratered skull. Flynn is sinking beneath the rim of the world of Wendy White, drifting down through the snow, so that she may bloom when things have melted, reemerge when it's warm, in a different driveway, drunk and fifteen years old, and no desire to have a name, to have a career, to have anything but the vibration and smooth roll of a skateboard beneath her feet.

She tilts her body as she heads up the half-pipe, shoots off the lip and twists, places her hand on the rim of the curve, willing all the strength of her arm to keep her up, her hair hangs down, her bent knees support the board, its wheels coasting in space.

The box is blasting Why can't I get just one kiss? Why can't I get just one kiss? Then the short, curve of the half-pipe again, A baby rocking to sleep in a cradle of concrete construction refuse. Maybe some things I wouldn't miss. This was the only thing besides reporting Flynn had ever felt she could make her body do.

Flynn would kill for five o'clock shadow but instead she wears her hair in a knot impaled with a blue proofing pencil, a frayed white oxford shirt and a man's black cardigan over top. Flynn would do this job for nothing. She would pay somebody else to be able to learn the things she learns. To gather information like the latchkey girl she was, tasting the apple core forgotten beneath the couch, reading every book, riffling through the desks and underwear drawers. She was in her element alone, moving, watching.

She loves that politicians lie. She loves her press pass with the city seal and signatures. She loves that cops leave blood and glass in the street and other cops let her get right up close to it. She loves that her profession is based in fact-checking. She loves that the paper's archive is called *a morgue*, and that the evening deadline is called *putting the paper to bed*. She loves turning the phrase that will lay everything bare, that will make the connections. Flynn gets paid to watch for subtleties, gets paid to be untrusted. To be ethical. To have hope. Because somewhere, she knows, there's a collective good. If people understand, if they get information, they will do the right thing.

And in that way, even a murder could be rectified, if people just knew more. Or if the prose were good enough, or if Flynn herself became harder, and colder, became a tomb around her own heart. She could drag everything to light. With enough research, and salacious detail and pretty words, she could slip meaning into public conversation, like slipping a pill into a dog's mouth by wrapping it in a piece of meat. This is how she earned her nickname. This is why she ran at dusk in the middle of winter, to get to a shallow grave before all the good light was gone.

―――――――

Four boys are peering into the car now. The oldest looks sad, the second oldest smirks. Sarah, chewing a wad of gum, blows a bubble that touches the glass then cracks like ice. They laugh and look at Flynn, to see if she'll laugh too, but this starts her crying again.

Flynn, Gabe says, rapping one knuckle on the glass. His voice muffled, It's eleven o'clock.

She wipes her face, says, I figured it was late.

Why don't you get out of the fucking *car* then? Jesse says.

Ah, you know, I'm planning on staying in the car, she says, and weeping has become like breathing.

She hears the storm door swing shut again and more crunching down the driveway and there's Joe in his Carhartt and fake-fur hat.

His children turn their rosy faces toward him, their white breathe rising, haloing his head. And they all, especially the girl, resemble him, dark brown eyes and round faces, high foreheads and messy hair, multiple copies of the same child.

Would you guys get the hell away from the goddamn car like

I ast you? He opens the back door and tosses in another rolled-up wool blanket and a bag of tortilla chips.

Thanks, Flynn tells him, still weeping.

He says, You got it kiddo, take your time.

I mean it, he says to the kids, Get. In. Side. They trudge up the driveway, defiant, hunching their shoulders as if they are actually disobeying him.

After the bars close, she watches loud college boys and quiet, slow-walking townies make their way back through the neighborhood in groups or solitary, coming from Anacones or Micky Rat's. They cross back into their own neighborhoods without a word to one another. A similar ritual was being carried out now on the Westside too, she knew. Only the parties crossing were drunken criminology majors and art therapy majors with lower SAT scores and less family income, passing by bandanna-wearing teenagers who wore less leather and, statistically, carried more firearms. She'd watched this ritual of passing, of crossing, on the evening she took her tape recorder down to the scene to have a walk-through with a strong squat cop whose voice had been playing in her head ever since.

All I can tell you now is they're being held for questioning 'cause of—

—eld for questioning 'cause of a report from neighbors that a loud—

—tioning because of a report from neighbors that a loud and disturbing noise was coming from, the apart—

—oise was coming from the apartment. This turned out to be an electric sander.

In the summer she'd take Joe's kids to a beach on Lake Erie; a crowded strip of public waterfront at the end of a narrow road near the remains of an abandoned amusement park. The sprawling skeleton of a rollercoaster jutted up, black and broken against the white sky, and she swam with them in water that she knew was contaminated, that she'd researched, she'd written about. But it was warm and got deep gradually, and they ran in the waves and dug in the sand, and there was nowhere else. Everyone swam there. Everyone had to die someday. To play by the ruins, and absorb your city's legacy, and to see the sublime order of the industrial skyline, intricate and sprawling like the guts of a giant machine—at least they'd have that.

On the way home in the car, the whole ungrateful brood of them would sing "Smells Like Teen Spirit," "This Land Is Your Land," "Fifteen Miles on the Erie Canal," and always "Dirty Old Town." It was something to hear their pretty voices, especially on "Dirty Old Town." When they'd pile out of her little car there'd be sand and dirt all over and the seats would be wet with their cheek marks.

—ten in the morning to check on the disturbance report and
found . . . here you can see where it . . . yeah . . . Ro
bance report and found . . . here you can see where it . . . yeah
. . . Roberts and Bectel sanding the living room floor.

It's still dark when Marie opens the door and sits in the back next to her. Flynn has been crying in her sleep, a constant, almost comforting state. Marie is wearing a nightgown and snow boots and a yellow puffy coat.

Boy. It's cold in here, she says, reaching into the bag of chips and eating one, talking with her mouth full. I guess you had a bad day, huh?

Flynn's eyes are nearly swollen shut. Marie eats another chip, tucks the blanket around Flynn, and keeps her hand on her shoulder. Are you warm enough, she says You know it's about three now?

Oh, is it?

Yeah, Marie says. You know, if you wanted, it's a lot warmer in the house.

No, that's okay, thanks.

Okay. Well, the laundry room door is open, so . . . Marie pats her on the leg and opens the car door. She says, You don't have to punish yourself. I know how you feel about Wendy White.

But she doesn't. Flynn hates Wendy White. Flynn despises Wendy White. Flynn wishes Wendy White had never been found.

———————

We're working closely with the cops, but it's kinda funny you know 'cause a
ow 'cause a lot of us were, like, this is gonna change our lifestyle having them around. Y—
them around. Y'know it's, like, man, They're here again we gotta put the b—
here again we gotta put the bong away, but they're, like—it's cool, we've got a—
s'cool, we've got something more important to—"

———————

Sometime before morning White actually shows up. White as a ghost. Looking back at Flynn from the front seat, her hands curved over the head rest. She's wearing a brown miniskirt, an orange turtleneck sweater, and a busted watch with a faux-leather band, the broken second hand ticks back and forth between the six and the seven. She looks as she did in her MISSING photograph and not as she did at four o'clock yesterday afternoon.

White smiles, happy, like they're on a trip together.

Hey Wendy, Flynn says, resigned now to her own collapse. She starts laughing and so does Wendy White; stops abruptly and Wendy does too and the hair on the back of Flynn's neck turn to ice. Flynn shouldn't be afraid, she been researching Wendy for months, still the girl is horrifying. She lacks the enculturation of the living, as if she's from some affectless, yet familiar tribe. She stares at Flynn and runs her hands over her own face and clothes, she smells like a grave.

C'mon, says Wendy, let's get a beer over to Anacones? It's prolly still open. She looks at her watch.

Nah, says Flynn, I'm planning on staying in this car. Nothing against Anacones, though, place is great. They sit quietly while the second hand ticks up and back. And finally Flynn says, Y'know, Anacones patronage is emblematic of the demographic shift in the Northeast.

Huh. No kidding, says White, What's that mean, more rich people moving in?

No, Flynn tells her, relieved to be in command of the conversation. The opposite. Bailey Avenue is moving two blocks this way every year.

It seemed like an appropriate thing to tell someone in White's improbable state.

You know what the rate of gunshot fatality is over there?

No.

High, says Flynn. In the African American and Slavic population, it's been growing 30 percent each year. Since this time last year there've been ninety-four firearms-related deaths and twelve deaths related to arson.

Well, let's go over to Essex Street then.

Yeah, great, says Flynn. And what'd you do the day they dug you up Wendy? Oh, I went back to the Essex Street Pub. Fucking brilliant.

White shrugs, I just think you should leave the car is all. Her flat drawl grates on Flynn and she wonders if there's a threat somewhere in that sentence. She starts weeping again—out of irritation this time. The frustration at not being left alone. She doesn't want to ask White any questions because they've all been answered by that dismembered mummy, in a summer print dress, which stared up from a cut in the earth swallowing the whole world. Turned out there was no mystery at all—a crack, a hole, and everything's exposed.

Finally, because Wendy won't leave and because Flynn is still more reporter than human, she asks, Was it just Roberts and Mike Bectel?

Yeah, says Wendy dully. Some of us were sitting out front of the Essex partying.

Flynn winces, she detests the word *partying*, sees euphemisms as a sign of mental weakness. She wants White to say, we were sitting out front snorting cocaine, or We were drinking beer and talking. There was no party anywhere, despite the recent graduation. They were three people with bachelor's degrees getting fucked up, and, she knows from interviews, talking about strip clubs over the bridge in Fort Erie and Roberts's new car. Hearing the word *partying* replaces her fear with a genuine sense of relief that White is dead. If Wendy White's death means Roberts and Bectel spend twenty years in prison, getting what they gave, that's okay with Flynn. If there are fewer women like Wendy White and fewer men like Roberts and Bectel every year, that's okay with Flynn. Fewer partiers, fewer

Canisius High School boys in their polo shirts with their baseball caps on backwards.

Afterwards, we went to the Elmwood Steakout and then back to Mike's. He had this little boxer puppy and it had shit all over the place and it really stunk and we were kinda laughing about that and then BAM. My face started bleeding, from like, nowhere, and then BAM, y'know, *again*. And I was like, oh fuck. Oh no. This was a mistake. And as I was falling, I remember thinking, I'm going to die and the last thing I'm gonna smell is dog shit.

But it wasn't, Wendy says. It was pine trees, like camping smells. Or maybe I smelled that today, when I first saw you. Man, you were sick, Flynn. I've never seen anyone get that sick.

Flynn wants White out of the car now. She's hates the girl for traumatizing her with the intimacy of her corpse, making her sit there in the car for eight hours like a zombie, for making her throw up at the site. She had Vicks on her upper lip and a handkerchief the cop had given her and she could barely breathe, so constricted was her chest. She couldn't think, couldn't write a word.

At twenty-three Flynn knows she'll never become a correspondent. She will never be a war reporter. She couldn't drive home because, thankfully, her car doors were frozen shut, and she had to call Joe for a ride. He took her back to the office to write the piece, then drove her home, but she wouldn't get out of the car. When he took her back to his place, she didn't follow him in, so he got her some blankets and went back inside.

Flynn has turned to dust in the back of an '87 Chevy parked in her editor's driveway on Lisbon Avenue, around the corner from Anacones, and it's fucking cold in that car now that White's ghost has showed up, and now she knows she is no one.

It's okay, White told her, but the ghost was wearing Flynn's disgust and distress on her own face.

You're a *woman*, the ghost told her, like she was trying to remember the word, breaking things down before she went on her way. You're a woman. Like I was. Like *me*. Like *I* was. She watches the breath pouring from Flynn's lips and opens the dark clean void of her own mouth but nothing comes out.

Flynn's body makes the fourth twist down into the concrete manger of the half-pipe. The point of upside-down waiting is the period at the end of the sentence, and she skates, sentence after sentence, swinging up, waiting weightless again—the top of her head poised above the hard cement. She wears cutoff Levi's and a man's A-shirt, no bra, combat boots with no socks. She's shaved one side of her head with dog clippers. One of her knees is deeply brush burned. The music is loud but there's no one to hear it for miles. When she sees pictures of this time, she recognizes only her eyes. All she wanted was to read books and drink beer, and skate. At fifteen she was still climbing trees and up onto abandoned factory roofs; still building forts, stealing people's lawn ornaments, eating candy for dinner. She had sex with her boyfriend in the attic when her parents were gone, surrounded by boxes of mildewed books, saved schoolwork, and broken furniture.

Sometimes she'd swim alone in the muddy and swollen river, staying close to the bank, her feet sinking into the silt. She wished White could have had that summer. Could take off the miniskirt and broken watch. But the idea of White sitting at a table with two preppie boys as they talked about the best place to see money stick to naked human skin makes her hate the dead girl all over again. Why did White sit there with them, at the edge of her grave? Why had she been there at all?

---

living room floor. They were trying to r—
ing to remove a dark stain about four by four and a half feet.
At this point officer Maitland and myself—
a dark stain with about four by four and a half feet. At this
point officer Maitland and myself informed Mr. Bectel and
Mr. Roberts of—
land and myself informed Mr. Bectel and Mr. Roberts of their
Miranda rights and—

Flynn has caught a chill. The sky is pale pink in the east and the windows of the car are covered with frost, frozen beads of condensation on the interior. She sits up and catches the reflection in the sideview mirror, it's Joe's salt-and-pepper cattle dog, standing beside the car looking back at her.

I've always hated you, says the dog.

Great, says Flynn. Now I'm the motherfucking Son of Sam.

The dog blinked and Flynn looked away from the mirror but it kept talking.

I could tell you didn't like me because I do tricks.

I don't think one way or the other about you, Gus.

I would bring a quarter for you to flip for me and you laughed.

Most dogs play fetch with a ball, she said.

I like the coin in my mouth, said the dog. And when you stopped throwing it, I wanted to bite you so you could feel my teeth in your skin.

Flynn closed her eyes.

When you feel my teeth, you'll do what I want. They're what makes me a dog.

I've got teeth too, Flynn said. That's not what makes you a dog.

You don't know how it is, Gus says.

I don't, Flynn says. I don't know what it is to be a dog and I don't fucking care.

Come out of the car, the dog says, so I can eat you before they wake up.

Flynn rolls her eyes at the dog's reflection.

Why would I leave the car if I know you are going to eat me?

Oh, says the dog.

Yeah, says Flynn, oh.

A rap on the window and it's Gabe, the oldest, holding a steaming mug in his bare hands. Clouds are moving rapidly across the sky. The gray light giving way to sun, and an intense clear blue, like the heart of a flame. Frost on the windshield gleams, beaming patterns like lace into the car's interior. His cheeks are red and the hair beneath his hat looks wet.

We're going sledding down to Chestnut Ridge, you wanna come? Well, anyway, he says before she can answer, we're taking this car 'cause Mom's using the other one to go to bingo, so . . .

She hears the storm door snap back and three little kids push into the back next to her smelling like soap, fighting over the bag of chips on the floor. Joe and the older boys tie the toboggan to the roof, scrape the windows, stomp their boots.

The Chevy cruises along like a boat in a sea of ice and concrete, and it's a forty-minute drive to Chestnut Ridge through the majesty of Great Lakes industrial land, through the bright sky and massive buildings, through the flat expanse that hints of water in the distance. The twins stare at her while they drive until Sarah points to the hills where they're heading and they look away.

The crest is long and steep, a gleaming white slope overlooking steel mills and granaries and ships on the cracked and frozen river. The river that Flynn knows contains eight thousand pounds of mercury and thirteen thousand pounds of sulfur dioxide dumped by Buffalo Dye and Color.

Flynn is trying to hold it together with the details. The names and dates and times. The locations and the descriptions of these locations that will bring things together in a neat package, the who-what-when-where. The facts that will prevent White's corpse from winning. White's corpse gets the Pulitzer, gets the last word. That discarded doll of her, zipped into a bag and hoisted onto a stretcher and driven slow through the snowy city in an ambulance that can take its time. Wendy's got it now, the envy of all humanity. Not only is she a woman, she's also dead. There goes White to accept her award, leaving Flynn, pulling at her car door, and trying to clear the smells of menthol and quick lime and spoiled meat from her sinus cavities. *I knew where they'd find you*, Flynn thinks to the back of the ambulance doors. *The foundation is laid in the details. Take my pen, take my notebook, take my tape recorder. I'll switch places with you*, she thinks to the gray skin. *I'd have known by the details, Wendy. I'd have known. I'd have lived.*

As her work at the paper became more automatic, she thought of herself like a bricklayer.

But nah, Joe told her, it's more like being a ball player—you're the ringer right now—hittin it outta the park and we all like that. But it's just *words*. It's just newsprint, Flynn. It ain't no fucking brick wall. People will be lining their bird cages with your story by the end of the day. Believe me, our effect on the material world is not what it seems.

––––––––––––

The parking lot is enclosed by pine trees, and small mountains of plowed snow, the tops covered in a thin layer of soot.

Joe pulls the hood of his Carhartt up and begins unlashing the sled from the roof, and then he and the boys carry it single file toward the cabin by the toboggan run.

The smaller kids get out of the car, mittened and pink-cheeked, stomping and kicking clumps of snow and ice. And then Flynn gets out. She's not dressed for it, has no hat, no mittens and her hair, now greasy, is plastered against her swollen face, her eyes raw and red.

She follows them up the long wooden stairs of the toboggan run, and they are waiting at the top so that she can be the first one on—crossed legs tucked up beneath the curve in the front of the sled. Sarah sits in the very back and sandwiched between them are all the boys. From the top of the run, she can see Bethlehem Steel like a vast, black, fenced-in city, like a castle glimpsed from a feudal home. Smoke unfurling, dark and cumulous from the stack into the bright gray air. And she has no more words for it. Just the sight of the majestic expanse as they race down the run.

Their bodies are warm at her back and her stomach is hollow with sensation and speed. Her face stung by ice. They scream together as one voice and the printed word is gone, gone, erased by the velocity and the snow. And it's like the half-pipe, only better and faster, and no slow-motion waiting. And they scream on the sled, and they sing while they walk it back up the hill.

And later in the car, mile after mile, flushed with sweat, their toes and fingers numb, they continue to sing. Why can't I get just one kiss? Why can't I get just one kiss? The voices of the twins and Sarah's clear vibrato-less soprano and the cracked baritones of Jesse and Gabe, Joe's bass the lowest common denominator; and her own smoker's alto, the mordent report, that ties it all together. Her narrow range hitting those same notes again and again, holding on in the middle precise and clear to that single diesis that is somehow never heard.

They sing Add it up. Add it up. Add it up.

STRIKE ANYWHERE

The boy wears thick elastic bracelets that fit snug on his wrists and forearms; casings from abandoned artillery shells he found by the fence. He used a nail to pull them off then pried loose the caps and poured the gunpowder into a pile, trying not to mix it with dust from the ground. It would burn better without the dust. His sweaty hair is full of dirt, tangled in the back on a thin strand of leftover ball chain from his Gidi's tags.

From the bunker the entire valley reveals itself; barbed wire fence, a road, a square field of cotton. The pines enclosing the apple orchard and even further the tops of industrial buildings in the town. The land that is untended looks like it has been set on fire. The trees are dry weeds and the ground mottled with patches of black and gray and yellow, the roof of the factory shines, white and untouched, reflecting the sun. From the bunker, he can hear everything—a bicycle coasting in the distance, the birds that come out at dusk. He can hear the sounds from yesterday—the scream and whomp that resonates through the body and through the body of the valley.

He pokes a stick into the crumbling concrete. It's hot and the smell of cow shit is rising from the pole barns below. Tonight, he'll ask Itai for matches.

The horizon is orange now and transports are coming back up the hillside and he spits and points the stick out at the road and closes one eye, whispering the word *stupid*. Gidi isn't down in the fields and won't be picking him up on the way to dinner. And he aims the stick at each truck in turn: pop, pop, pop until they're out of sight and the sky is dark red and then purple. It's a long time to wait for nothing.

Gidi spoke no English and said he didn't want to hear it. But the boy could read a bit. He could sing along to the BBC. Fake English was fine, made everyone smile. Gidi spoke better than the other men, because he used proper words, older words, he spoke better than the boy's mother, because he never used slang. He had smooth dark skin and dark eyes and rolled the white box of cigarettes into the sleeve of his T-shirt. Before he left, he'd shaved his long hair close to his head.

The boy had a quiet spot picked out for the gunpowder, a flat stretch of sidewalk to set it up. Before he'd found the second box of buried shells, he was planning on writing "Gidi" but now he could spell the whole name, draw pictures, set the hills on fire. The future was full, was a junkyard of everything that could happen. When he came home, they could drive down to the cotton in the jeep, and eat salad for breakfast on the bench outside the storage shed. They could eat chocolate, they could have birthdays.

The boy kicked stones free from the concrete and slid down to the smooth path following the glow-in-the-dark stripes painted on the walkway, running as it got darker; the thought of ending up in the wrong place made the hair on his arms stiff, electric, and the noise of nightbirds and insects was no comfort. He didn't slow down until he could he see the shadows of the other boys, walking together; the young guards, in their blue shirts. He knew Itai by his walk and cut across the dirt road, jumped the trench instead of crossing on the boards, nearly stumbling on the cushion of the sod lawn, then fell in line, putting an arm around the other boy's shoulders.

What's this? Itai says. Evel Knievel? Go get your shirt.

Why?

Go put on your blue shirt.

The boy is the youngest, but not the smallest. Itai is seven and two inches taller but thin, he doesn't have the body to tell the boy what to do.

No. It's okay like this.

It's not, Itai says, taking the boy's hand, spinning him around. He says, I'll race you. But doesn't let go of him.

They run hand in hand, trying to get ahead of each other, until Itai is leading, nearly dragging him, nearly pulling him to his knees. The branches of the lemon trees outside their empty house are heavy with fruit and its dark and cold in the hallway and it smells like bleach. Their low rubber boots squeak as they scuff around in the gloaming, looking for the yellow toy tractor hanging from the ceiling by a chain. The boy yanks it, flooding the white-tiled room with light and they squint until it doesn't hurt. The windows are covered with cardboard, the curtains are closed, all the beds are neatly made. The boy opens his drawer; nothing in it but the blue shirt. He opens Itai's drawer, nothing in it at all.

Is it laundry? he asks.

Itai shrugs.

The boy grabs the blue shirt and pulls it on over Evel Knievel. Have you still got those matches? he asks.

Itai makes a short sucking sound behind his teeth.

You used them all? the boy asks. Hasn't your mother matches at her apartment?

Hasn't *your* mother?

She doesn't smoke.

Why not?

Get them, says the boy, and I'll show you where to dig for shells.

Itai jumps down from the dresser. Pulls the light chain and they run across the wet lawn to the dining room and heave open the heavy wooden door. All the young guards are there. The whole room packed, each group at a different table. Four-year-olds sitting on the floor; the high school group sits smoking on a bench near the kitchen, long-haired boys and their girlfriends, in blue shirts and flared jeans and clogs. They're sure to have lighters.

Everyone's voice is lost in murmurs. The boy's group sits in the back by the pebbled wall beneath framed photographs of their grandparents in gray tank tops, leaning on shovels and pick axes. He climbs onto the chair and swings his feet.

Avi pours water for their group and he says, They're coming back. That's why we're here with the shirts.

A shock to his stomach, and the boy's whole body is a beating heart. He snaps his bracelets against his wrist under the table, one by one, and looks up at a picture of his mother's father standing in a field of mud. That's where they're sitting now, where all that dirt was.

A whole unit. They're probably with our mothers right now, waiting to come in and see us.

A whole unit of what? asks the boy, and he makes Avi's voice say paratroopers, in his head.

A unit from the front, Avi says, pushing his glasses up on his face, his fingernails are dirty and his lips are ringed with something purple, someone gave him candy, there must be candy. I heard them say "a whole unit," he said pointing to the older boys, I think that's what they're talking about.

Avi's father had come home last month, picked him up from school, still wearing his uniform, and carried him home. He carried him, an eight-year-old, like a baby. The next day they caught Avi by the fish pond and made him fight Itai. His nose bled, and they told him what he was for getting beat by a seven-year-old and threw his glasses out into the grass. They'd have thrown them into the pond but he was their friend.

You don't know anything, the boy says. We're here to take rifles apart.

We don't do rifles until the first day of the week, Avi tells him, not mad at anyone.

The boy whispers paratroopers and wants to say it out loud for good luck so he says, Paratroopers are the toughest.

All of them are the toughest, Itai says, repeating the words their teacher uses to break up fights.

She looks like a boiled frog, Levi says of their teacher.

A boiled, puking frog, says Gilad.

No, but paratroopers, the boy says, have M-16s and M-16s are better than Uzis.

Not true, Levi says.

True, says the boy. Uzi is not a big gun. He snaps his bracelets under the table to the rhythm of a song by Aris San.

They're all good guns, Itai says.

The debate calms the boy, he's never changed his mind on the subject of M-16s. He drinks a cup of water, thirstier than he realized. Any minute Gidi's unit will walk in the door. And Gidi and Itai's father will come over to their boys and pick them up. And take them home, and let them sleep on the couch in their parents' apartments.

Gidi will walk across the lawn in his sneakers and jeans with a cigarette tucked behind his ear. No, he wouldn't walk, he would be running still in his uniform; he'd tell the boy's mother he could see her later and run straight to the children's house to look for him, and when he didn't find him, he'd rush to the dining room. He'd spot the boy at once and open his arms and the boy would jump down from his chair. And they would walk out together, and they wouldn't have to sing "Arise Ye Prisoners of Want." And the boy would carry his gun. And when they saw his mother she would say, You look even more like him now that you're six. You look exactly like him.

But Levi's aunt was standing at the front of the dining room, dressed in army pants and boots, the strap of her rifle on her shoulder, her hand in the air to quiet them, and it was dark. If Gidi came through the doors he might not see him right away.

We're here to go over the rules for extended stay in shelters, Levi's aunt says, and now they are quiet.

See? says the boy, It's another practice.

Shut up, Itai shoves him.

Tomorrow we will be underground where it is safe and comfortable. All of your things have been packed. Your books, your homework. But tonight, when we finish, you'll go to your parents as a special treat.

The boy cracks his knuckles.

They sing. It's not Aris San. It's No one will give us deliverance, neither God nor King nor Hero. It's We will achieve liberation with my own hand.

When it's over Itai asks if they have packed his marbles.

Of course, Levi's aunt says. You think we're barbarians?

I want you now to look around at your friends, she says. And they look at each other, look across the room in the dim light. The white laces on the fronts of their shirts shine. It's a sea of blue and dark hair, and some glinting reflections from glasses. The boy thinks about horses in the coral and chickens packed in crates, and of the wild boar that ran tearing up the field. He pretends to light a match.

Now look at your own group, she says.

And the boy holds Itai's hand under the table.

We are who we rely on, Levi's aunt says.

———————————

His mother has made cake and the house is lit with candles, and there's newspaper over the windows and it smells like her clothes and like onions. She says the words he imagined her saying . . . now that you are six, and watches him eat and drink watery red fruit punch, wipes her nose.

. . . your pajamas, okay?

He shoves the second piece of cake into his mouth and it makes her laugh.

She reaches for him and he climbs into her lap and shuts his eyes and she brushes his hair back from his forehead, she is warm and her voice is only a sound.

. . . gets home and we'll . . .

He curls deeper into her lap, resting his head on her chest. She carries him to the bathroom, turns on the shower. There's a lit nub of a candle in there and the little window looks out to moonlight, and there must be matches in the house somewhere. She puts the lid of the toilet down and sits, holding him still while the steam rises and their shadows flicker.

Arms up, she says, pulls off the shirts, untangles the ball chain from his hair and sets it on the sink. He stands and he takes off his jeans. It's cold and he doesn't want to be wet or have soap in his hair and he climbs back into her lap naked, his skin pale next to her dark arms.

At the children's house they take showers together in the evening, and no one dresses or undresses them. He wouldn't want Itai or Levi seeing him now, sitting on his mother's lap.

She pulls back the curtain so he can stand under the warm water, washes his back with a soapy cloth. Runs her hands over his hair and then scrubs with her nails. She washes his dirty hands and fingernails and wrists, rubbing soap over his bracelets to clean the dust from of them. Then stands by the shower wiping her long wet hair away from her face. While the gray water runs into the drain.

Is a whole unit coming home? he asks her.

No, she says. Not yet.

I heard a whole unit of paratroopers is coming home.

Hm, she says. Who told you that?

A mouse, he says.

A mouse, ah, but is she reliable?

She used to live in a F-15.

A mouse plane?

No, for people. And she said a whole unit.

Wah alla, where did you meet her, this mouse?

He put his foot over the drain, watched the soap and dirt pooling in the bottom. Near Qasr Al Hayr. She said they're coming home.

So far away, I didn't know you'd been that far away.

I was stationed there, the boy says.

Last week?

Yeah, he says, that's where I was. It's a castle.

The living room floor is cold. His mother wraps him in a towel and hands him pajamas, but he gives them back for her to dress him. He unfolds the sheets on the couch quickly and climbs up, tucks his feet into the cushions. The duvet is heavy and she lies beside him, strong and warm. The black-and-gold demitasse cups on the kitchen shelf shudder in the light of the flame, but there are no matches that he can see. Her voice is quiet and he closes his eyes, puts his arms around her neck, his ear to her lips.

You are my little fish, she says, my little antelope, you are the Indian ocean.

The smell of the snuffed candle is thick in the air and the voices of the jackals ring up from the valley, crying like they're wounded, yipping like they've won.

———————

Gidi came to live there because it was dangerous where he was from, but you couldn't see how dangerous from pictures; cars, houses made from wood, green grass, maple trees, buildings like towers; Gidi on a blanket on the beach. And the streets in the pictures were wide and paved and there were squirrels. Gidi had another name then, he said, a name he didn't pick himself.

It's not dangerous underground. It's like a cave and the bunks swing down hard on their hinges and stop at the end of the chain, each foam mattress covered with a white sheet and a wool blanket.

Shira yells top but the boy climbs up before she can.

I called top bunk, she says.

I'm *in* the top bunk, he tells her.

Tsipi plays cards with Itai, sitting cross-legged on the floor. Shira talks about her dog and how when she turns eight she'll work in the horse stables with her mother.

You can bring your dog with you to the stables, she says.

Big deal, Itai says. You can bring your dog anywhere.

Not to the kitchen, she says.

Levi and Yarden are lying on blankets on the floor while their group helper, a rangy teenage boy with black ringlets, tells them a story, between drags on his cigarette. He has matches. Or a lighter. He must have a lighter.

He's telling them about the last day of induction. How when they turn ten, they'll go together, with their backpacks, and they'll follow a map to a place outside the fence ten kilometers from here.

Syria? Itai asks, and the girls laugh.

The map has only numbers instead of places, the group leader says. And the numbers tell you what kind of land is around, whether it's a hill or a lake or a group of trees. If you read it wrong you can get off course.

Did you read it wrong?

We read it wrong all the time. They gave us one backpack that had all the water and food in it for the whole group and we gave it to just one guy to carry, and because we got lost a couple of times, he got really mad, carrying the heaviest things. Who could blame him? What did we do wrong?

You thought he was a donkey, said the boy.

Right, we did, we treated our friend like a donkey, we were so dumb. But then we divided up the food and water and everybody carried some of the heavy things and some of the light things. We walked in a big circle and that's how we figured out our mistake with the map. And then two hours later we were there.

Where?

He sucked his teeth. Can't tell you. It's a secret place.

The boy leans over the side of the bunk to listen better.

After we finished that hike, we laid down our camp and set a fire. And then we were part of the movement, we could go far—fifteen- and twenty-kilometer hikes—and take trips down south in the desert. Where it's so quiet like you can't believe and the air ripples and the sky is not like here at all.

The children sit closer, right at his feet.

If you come from the city, he says, you don't know how to do anything. You don't know how to hike or read maps or do things that you already know—how to take guns apart in the dark, or how to hide or track or find water. Think about what it would be like to be eighteen years old and not know how to find water. This is why we're the best. We're not the ones who get killed.

The boy's stomach hurts. He snaps at his bracelets, looks up at the thick metal door. It's cold and the walls feel rough and damp but there's smooth paint in places beside the bunks—paintings of tropical fish and coral and sea anemones; paintings of flowers, and there's a pink-nosed mouse. He runs a finger over the surface; purple and gold and red and blue, smooth and cold like ice. It's a cave painting.

When he jumps off the bunk the bottoms of his feet sting, numb from landing so hard. He pushes into Itai and wrestles him around on the floor and once he's pinned, he whispers the word *matches* and Itai ducks his head in a quick nod.

When the bombing is over, Levi's aunt comes and opens the door; a shadow with the sun blazing behind her, and then there is her smile. She pats the group helper on the back, tells them to pack their things, put all the laundry in a pile by the door of the children's house. But they rush past her into the smell of grass and soot, squinting.

The sun has crested the top of the tree and they run out to the sod lawn and jump over the trench back and forth and back and forth. Itai and the boy run to the shed beside the children's house for bikes. They ride the dirt road that circles the dining room, racing along uphill, standing to pedal, they follow the edge of the fence, coasting the long dust road to the front gate, and stop at the crumbling bunker to rest. Beneath them it looks like the fields have already been harvested. There are black holes in the road to town. The white factory is half there, the rest of it smudged into the dirt. They look only for a short time before riding on, up the big hill to Itai's mother's apartment. She's not there so they eat sugar cubes from the bowl on the table. The boy rummages in the closet for a plastic bag, stuffs it into his pocket. Itai searches the cupboard for more sugar cubes, and finding another stash fills his pockets, but the boy doesn't care. He's pulling out the drawers in the coffee table, he pushes a chair to the counter so he can climb up and reach the cupboard above the stove, and at last he finds them. Two boxes. Strike Anywhere.

Just below the surface, the ground is full of mortar shells and rounds and smaller bullets. Itai rakes his hand through the dirt and laughs. They push everything they can find into one pile and divide it up.

The boy puts his rounds into the bag to carry back to his gunpowder pile and take apart.

Itai is pulling the casings off the mortar rounds and twisting them around his wrist. He holds it up next to the boy's to compare.

Don't tell anyone else, the boy says. Or just, you can tell Shira.

Itai nods, gives the boy the box of matches and takes out his own. He pries the cap from a bullet and spills a tiny black dot on to the ground, strikes the box. The flame sparks and hisses and a thin line of smoke rises into the clouds. The boy pries off another and makes the letter Alef on the ground in gunpowder, sets the edge on fire watching the flame travel quickly around the letter and flare out.

Wah alla, Itai says. It's nice.

The boy smiles.

We can find a way to fire those mortars, Itai says.

The boy sucks his teeth. If we ask older boys, they'll take them from us.

We can say we just found a couple, Itai says, bring them one, they'll show us how. They'll let us watch.

Tomorrow, says the boy, tying his plastic bag to the handlebars of the bike.

It's hard to keep the bike straight, and he rides swerving along the edge of the fence, pulled by the weight of the bullets, nearly falling when he looks back to see Itai crouching above a bright fire.

One full bag of gunpowder with string tied in triple knots around the top. Half a box of matches. Five drawings. He is thoroughly washed and combed and he kicks his feet against the legs of the chair. Snaps the elastic at his wrists. He is six and a half and he knows that Gidi is now thirty-two.

Is he thirty-two or thirty-two and a half? he asks his mother.

She laughs. She has been laughing all day at everything he says. She smiles at him and doesn't answer, flips through a magazine.

Thirty-two or thirty-two and a half?

Mmm? she looks up as if he had never said anything. Then says, Thirty-two.

I'm going out, he says.

She smiles so wide, her eyes so shiny that he stares at her in suspicion until she laughs again.

What are you looking at? she says, Go ahead, go.

The sky is a clear, bright blue, their mothers aren't working and they all have off from school.

He heads straight to his gunpowder and lugs it to the flat stretch of sidewalk by his mother's door. It's heavier than it looks and he's already sweaty and dirty again by the time he gets it to the spot, then he sits in the sun and rests, one arm bent over his head shading his eyes. It smells like flowers and the banana tree in the front yard looks even bigger and sloppier than last year; its trunk a stringy mess. He gazes up as a helicopter passes low over the cluster of one-story stucco houses. Then turns his back to the sun and sets to work.

It's a strange name, those backwards letters. He pulls a small piece off the corner of the plastic bag and begins to slowly pour. He has it all written in black, not quite right, but you can read it.

He turns, sits in front of the gunpowder to hide it, feels in his pocket for matches. Another helicopter passes. And the sun is so hot it burns his arms, makes his eyes heavy. The heat ripples like water above the road in the distance, and there are the sounds of jeeps. Of voices. People have been getting dropped off all day.

He is almost dozing when he hears the creak of an emergency break being pulled. Nearly beyond his sight a group of men step down from beneath the canvas hood of a personnel carrier and embrace, their guns slung on their backs. The boy is standing, though he doesn't remember getting up. He knows this man's step. Sees his shoulders square in the uniform. He stands rail straight on the walkway, awake but unable to move his feet.

Gidi's hair has grown out and the boy can see from a distance that he's grown a beard, that his skin is darker and beneath the sun his uniform has faded to the color of dust. His teeth are white amid the black hair, like an animal's, and as he runs toward the house, the boy pulls out his matches and turns to the name. A scrape and a pop and he lights the edge of the L jumping back from the flame so that his father can see it racing along.

LARRY GREENBURG it blazes, hissing and popping and sending thick black smoke into the summer sky.

Look Gidi! the boy shouts, dancing, his fists clenched at his sides. I wrote your name in gunpowder! And the man is there now, grabbing him. He kneels and kisses him on the face and runs big hands over the boy's hair, closes his fists around the fine brown curls and rests his forehead against the boy's shoulder. This father, this man, is huge, arms hard, a chest of stone inside a dirty uniform. He smells of sweat and cigarettes, his hair full of fine dust and the boy puts his hands in his father's beard, on his hair, he tries to rub it clean, rests his forehead against the man's. The smell of sulfur is overpowering as the separate streams of smoke rise from each letter and come together above their heads in one black column that continues to rise.

And this man, this father, takes deep breaths and holds them, and he whispers in English, the same unintelligible words over and over, breathing and holding his breath. Breathing and holding his son's small body to his chest.

I wrote your *name*, Aba, the boy says. I wrote your name in gunpowder.

HISTORY LESSON

1

Those last years in the city, when people would pay for a human voice to put them to sleep at night, when people would pay for a human voice to tell them how to breathe, I was dying for a silence that was no longer possible. And not even the ghost of the landscape, the ghost of the neighborhood remained. We were not watching things carefully in those last years, we were keeping our heads down and pretending there was a future. We were amassing the resources we'd need to break the gravitational pull. No one anticipates how fast change happens. By the time the perimeter fences went up it just looked like more construction.

2

I watched him as he slid a tie around his neck in that room in an empty tenement with electricity running through an extension cord from the building next door, not even knowing it was a sanctuary.

There's no one left inside those borders now who could receive this message; a codex buried in the sand, for when we're gone, something to refute the false history of helplessness and virtue; the story of how they built seed banks reinforced like bunkers to protect the germ of the world, or how they raised sea walls, grew food under acetylene lamps, made hajj to see the last of the ice.

In Alphabet City we watched the fires become gardens, but we were never stupid enough to think the place wouldn't burn again. If you'd ever lost at anything, you'd have known when it was time to go.

3

That first disease, what an opportunity; no more ancient rituals on the pier, no more disgrace to the family. And those people who took the apartments of the dead had such robust health, their eyes gleaming and souls half there.

In time they'd come to eat flour made from insects, replace their failing hearts with the hearts of pigs. They would huddle in cool towers around their devices, watching aerial footage of vineyards on fire, orange as a forge, forests reduced to charcoal.

They said no one could have predicted the disease that followed the disease.

4

Before the fire, the burial, the flood, when we couldn't come out to work on the machines because of the wind, Allen Street was a ditch and the workers camped at the edge of the neighborhood and were paid to demolish their own homes and build towers for people who sold them poisoned milk. There are herds of deer there now, their hooves clicking on the hard concrete.

5

It was once someone's job to supply schools across the country with sealed plastic packets of fetal animals so that their private anatomies could be observed by children; the dainty doll version of intestines, the heart the size of a finger joint; blood vessels like ruby-colored fishing line.

Someone drove around in a van with all those vacuum-packed cadavers. As an artist I am versed in the creation and preservation of material things. In the survival of matter, of form.

Blood lasts longer on canvas than it does in your veins.

6

In Exarchia I buy a pair of pony skin shoes, and incense from the kiosk, and liquor made from the tears of trees, and toothpaste made from myrrh, and regulation masks against tear gas and against the windstorms blowing in from the Sahara.

I buy the tentacles of an animal that was as smart as a child and lived as long as my uncle and eat them in the evening by the locked front gate.

The white sprawl of Athens is a sea of terraces, TV antennas, and satellite dishes, there are chunks of mountain and forest; climbing vines and houses built into the cliffside, hollows below street level that shelter byzantine churches; foxes burrowing in the cedars on Lycebettus, flocks of finches roosting in the eaves of modernist arcades. There is no better place to be lost than a place that has already been lost.

7

Cars smolder at the border of the neighborhood, beneath black flags, like a warning. Below the barbed wire on the roof of Gare Squat a banner reads: We will not end the occupation. We will trample you.

Up on Kalidromiou it smells like neroli and a burning car and the man from the shoe repair's got dark-stained hands, which I notice when he locks the gate. When I ask him if he saw the people throwing molotovs at the police bus last night he shrugs and says, The kids have to practice somewhere.

8

We slip past the bitter orange trees and through the narrow street, clang up the metal steps to drink cold mastica from little cups. From above we can see how lithe their bodies are, how smart they're dressed, bandanas up over their faces.

A breeze moves the hedge of jasmine that climbs the building, and blossoms pool in gutters already white with ash.

They are flipping the car, I say, to practice the language.

They have flipped the car, he corrects.

RETOUCH/SWITCH

She talked about money and how she didn't have any. Said she was terrified of losing her job but the truth was she didn't need it. The job was retouching; making skin look smooth, flesh lean, eyes bright, faces pale. She talked about the crime of it. How it wrecked your head. How you wanted more. She swore it was the money that kept her there. Money made our lips full and rosy, our bellies smooth and taut, our thighs slimmer, sanitized our forms of the moments that built us.

Her eyes were gray like concrete, and she never said I. She said we. We can't sleep at night, she said. We're hungry again, she said.

She sent pictures of herself alone, and said this is a picture of us.

Sent pictures of horses, pictures of parking lots, pictures of an open wound, a pocked stone. Here we are, she said. And here we are again.

She said when she lay beside me she retouched me in her mind. Those eyebrows the wrong shape, that lip too thin. Arms should be slimmer, breasts higher, no one has a birthmark like that.

When she came to me in Aveyron, I'd been alone for months, not speaking to anyone. The town was surrounded by fields of yellow rapeseed flowers, elder trees bloomed their hot breath out into the empty courtyard. I'd been eating one meal a day.

There were white horses grazing and black moths clinging to the screen doors and kingdoms of frogs in the mud. And I was silent, ecstatic in the cradle of real things.

I'd left the States and the noise of people talking about who they were. I'd left the tyranny of their camera-ready faces. It was when people began to say they were "on brand" that I lost the power to speak. I left because there was nowhere to rest your eyes and because at home in solitude, a machine stared back at me. I left because I had nothing to say to anyone who stayed.

I loved her because she knew the membrane between this world and that one was thin.

That one, fairyland.

The smell of his skin.

Bent over, the fur of him, the knots in his spine, the flesh and meat of his ass. His face in the pillow, the weight of his body. The sound of his breathing like suffering. The salt musk alkaline smell and taste of him. Smell like mango, moldering pages, linseed oil, leather, ice.

His back streaked red and the stretchmarks at his shoulders where new muscles pushed against the skin and made tears in his body.

When he was her, she said she wanted to turn me inside out.

In the apartment above the bar. In the closet at work.

In the basement when she first lost her job.

She said it was like biting into a plum. It was like running fast down a hill so light you might become airborne.

Asleep in her studio. Asleep on the couch by my desk. Asleep near the ruin. In her bed—nothing else in the apartment; no furniture, not a scrap in the kitchen, a single bottle of fig leaf perfume in the medicine cabinet. On the beach, her hair bleached white in the sun. In the ramble. Asleep on the lawn in the park when the hawk came down to strike beside me, so close a clod of earth from its claws struck my face. And she brushed it away.

Driving with her in summer while her wife cried in the back seat. Each of us retouched by her.

Back in the States where I can't taste a thing, and your heart is a little coffin that you've lined for me with satin.

For a time, I lived alone where things grew everywhere; there were shale cliffs and waterfalls, rich moss and beds of fern along the forest floor. Long dead industrial buildings perched at the edge of the gorge, their roofs cratered and trees growing sideways from their walls.

You could scale the cliffside if you were light, you could stand on the roof, you could jump from the ruins into a deep pool the width of a fat man's body. Touch the bottom to bring up fistfuls of silt and stones and bullet casings and fossils.

There is solace in the long-abandoned place; in the golden hour. No one's voice and no one's touch to intercede between you and the world.

I lived here quietly, until another showed up, butch this time, a marathoner.

People thought his house was haunted because the TV antennas were from the fifties, and the doors swung open and slammed shut in the wind. And the barn looked like it had been smashed by a giant fist. I loved how he ruled this emptiness, and he knew it called to me like no other.

But inside there were more objects still, and he, chief among them, cultivating his body. David with a Gorgon's head.

It didn't matter who you were. I wanted nothing more than you.

We slept together on the Greyhound bus and shared our clothes and people had no shame in asking what we were.

Were we this or were we that? Cruising or sleeping out, safer together. The music loud from the street and the city sprawling white below us. You were the purest form. The one I liked best.

Our devotion and our poverty and our whole future clear.

You were the only thing that stood between me and nothing.

And we went down to the canal where those little boats were moored and crept inside one of them to sleep. The light from the flares and the light from the fire burned all night.

I left you with your hand pressed against the glass.

I left you amid the noise of the terminal.

That first time—the rush of bare life—the ecstatic loneliness. Like the world was going to tear right through me at last. You were the door in the dollhouse that led to the kingdom of the real.

You were the one. You were the only one.

If I could have left you forever I would.

DeCHELLIS

I left Willet Falls to live by the inlet between a hobo jungle and a man who used his money to keep two acres of Christmas lights shining all year long. The sky above the town was a blank white gray, and at night the glow from the field of life-size nativity scenes and fairy-lit trees blazed in the dark like searchlights or arson. I had come to Burdett because my uncle was headed back to court and the rest of my family had jobs and couldn't take the time.

When I got to Gordon's place, he was standing on the porch with an elegant gray-haired man named Johnny. And though I hadn't called or texted or emailed, neither of them were surprised to see me. Gordon was telling Johnny about the last time he'd been in the hospital. How he'd picked up a bed and thrown it across the room.

Hospital beds are very light, Johnny said.

Kylie, Gordon said by way of greeting, hospital beds are heavy right?

I said, Uh, yeah.

They're not, Johnny said. Tiny little nurses crank them with a crank.

Gordon was wearing a cardigan over his basketball jersey, and he'd grown a little paunch since I'd last seen him, but it takes a lot for someone that tall to look fat. His beard had grown out and his dark eyes were clear, he looked like he was coming round to the fact that I was standing in his yard.

He said, What's wrong Lollipop? You in trouble?

Gordon's latest round in rehab was paid for by the newspaper, but after he was arrested for walking other people's dogs, they didn't hire him back. He'd been spending his unemployment checks on dollhouse furniture again.

I said, No, everything is great. I got my pesticide handler's license finally, so could make more money, and that's why I could afford to visit. Plus with the case coming up . . .

Johnny frowned when I mentioned court.

Gordon told Johnny how I used to put a brick on the back of the riding mower to keep it from automatically shutting off. I didn't weigh enough, he explained, for the machine to believe someone was using it.

Machines don't *believe* anything, Johnny said.

Gordon said, Kylie, remember when I was strong and you were thin and I would wrench a door open just a crack so you could slip in and unlock it for us?

I do, I said.

But I didn't. I remembered him carrying me up Gun Hill when I was too skinny to stand. He saw me in the bookstore and said it didn't look like I was well enough to be out. I remembered him making me eggs. I remembered him drinking tumblers of vodka and refusing to wear anything but underwear and basketball goggles, and then my father saying I had to come back and live at home again.

You here to spy on us? Johnny asked.

No, I said, I thought I could find work here, which wasn't true at all. I was there to make sure Gordon didn't end up in jail or living in a tent full of two-inch-high tables and chairs and grandfather clocks down by the inlet, feeding fake porridge to fake mice with tiny silver spoons.

Johnny and Gordon exchanged a pitying look.

I don't need to *stay* with you, I said, and told them about the place I'd found near Coward's Christmas Wonderland.

Kylie, Gordon said, remember when your bike got stolen and you called the police and talked in the *Sling Blade* voice and we had to go look for it ourselves?

That was hilarious, I said. But I couldn't place it.

Remember when you got accepted to Julliard and you sent *them* a rejection letter? he laughed. But there was no reply to that one.

Johnny said he wasn't there to watch us go traipsing down memory lane, and before he left Gordon gave him a bottle of Dom Perignon the size of a pen cap, which was made of glass and sealed with a real cork.

Stay for tea, Gordon said to me. Chad will be happy you're here.

Inside the old house things were the same. Gordon's stand-up bass took up most of the living room. An orchestra of miniature instruments lay scattered atop the upright piano, and a box full of antlers that had been there since I was ten sat in the corner of the room next to a stack of newspaper clippings from when he wrote for *The Sentinel*.

A picture of my mother hung above the mantle and everything except the dollhouse furniture was covered in a layer of dust.

I got myself a glass of water and stood by the back window drinking it. Berry bushes and wild roses had eaten the garage. The kitchen was cluttered with the remains of breakfast and smelled like pancakes and chocolate. A tiny replica of the kitchen table sat on top of the kitchen table. This belonged to Chad. It was covered with a red and white checked tablecloth. A miniature newspaper lay on top, open to the sports section, and beside that a china cup and saucer, and a sugar bowl the size of a cherry pit.

Chad's little chair was empty.

I don't know where he's gone off to, Gordon said.

I said, Probably still at work, and watched my uncle's face come alive. That smile.

Kylie, You and me are peas in a pod.

My new place was a room in a double-wide with a hot plate and a plug-in kettle. The ground around the trailer was swampy and the air smelled of wood smoke.

How's he doing? my father asked, his voice cutting in and out from bad reception. How's the furniture situation?

Rain on the metal roof sounded like someone was trying to bury the trailer in gravel. Through the window I could see the glowing mechanical reindeer raising and lowering their heads as if startled by the step of a hunter.

Fine, I said.

Was Johnny there?

No.

He have a lawyer for walking them people's dogs?

Of course, I said.

He musta scared the hell out of them people. He could go away, you know. This isn't fighting or shoplifting no more.

He did those people a favor, I said.

Oh, here we go, said my father.

The other tenant of the double-wide was named DeChellis. He offered me a cigarette when I came out of my room. The kerosene stove was lit, and a pair of wet wool socks were draped over it, steaming into the air around us. I said, No thanks.

You Gordon Swank's daughter?

His niece, I said.

I stood in front of the stove and let it warm me. The socks smelled like a farm or a dog and the sound of the rain made us hunch as if we'd been struck by the cold weight of it.

There was a folded-up tarp, some duffle bags, and a blanket piled in a corner by the door, and it dawned on me that the double-wide was actually part of the hobo jungle; the fancy part.

You used to live up there in that house with him, DeChellis said. Didn't you go to Burdett High?

The school stood on a scrubby chunk of clear-cut land with woods on three sides and a highway running past, and the playing fields flooded all spring.

I said, No, I didn't, because I didn't want to hear about some relative of his who went there too and remembered me.

Sure, DeChellis said, they called you Lollipop, 'cause you were like a big head on a stick body. He exhaled a cloud of smoke, picked at a long yellow toenail. When he looked back up at me his long hair fell away from his face, he bit absently at his moustache.

You're thinking of someone else, I said.

Nah, I remember. Gordon Swank came to pick you up that once wearing pink running tights and beat the living piss outta some boy you used to date. Didn't you get a scholarship to opera school?

I said, All of that sounds like something you made up.

But he didn't make it up. And now I remembered him. His mother ran a beauty salon out of their house. And his father worked at Banfield Baker where they sold pellet fuel and grass seed and they had a monkey in a cage that died from choking on a quarter. Dechellis had represented France in the Model UN.

The windows in the paneled living room were fogging, and it wasn't day anymore, and the tiny lights from Coward's flickered through the downpour.

He's goin' t'jail this time, Lollipop. DeChellis said. Doesn't matter who you're related to or what people remember. You think I don't know why you're here?

Outside, the rain had let up some and the air was damp and cold. The trailer's cinderblock step sunk into the marshy ground, and I let the door snap back, and the double-wide shuddered. I walked directly to the edge of Coward's Christmas Wonderland and slipped below the electric fence without touching it. Between the luminous trees there was nothing but a black void. Peepers called to one another in the dark, and I could hear the water rushing in the inlet, the rustling of animals. Inside the fence the top branches of trees glowed with tiny white lights like a swarm of nesting fireflies. My boots made a sucking sound in the mud and a deer bolted from somewhere behind me braying out a wheezing rasp as it flashed past.

Joseph and Mary's shelter was damp and baby Jesus was as big as a real baby and lying in a real trough. If no one had been there to look out for him, he might have been eaten by the donkey. I went inside and sat on the floor. In the corner of the shelter a single red light from a surveillance camera beamed down on me, and soon I could hear the sloshing step of someone approaching.

This is private property, a voice called out.

Hello, I called back, I'm getting out of the rain.

Coward hunched down to see who was talking and the lights in the distance haloed his head and I could tell he was holding a gun though I couldn't yet see it.

That fence is here to keep you out, he said.

Me specifically?

People tell you not to be smart to a man alone at night, or to one holding a gun, or to men in general, but everyone knows it's really a roll of the dice.

When I stepped out of the shelter Coward's shoulders slumped and he looked like he might cry. The rain had turned to mist, rolling through the air around us.

My lord, Kylie Swank, he said, calling me by my mother's maiden name. You living in the Jungle?

I shook my head, pushed wet hair back from my shoulder.

You look just like your mama, he said. Thought I was seeing a ghost.

When I got to Gordon's the next morning, Chad was standing by a tiny door cut into the baseboard, by the bottom of the stairs. He had a shocked expression on his face but that was just the way his eyes were painted. Chad was wearing a white button-down shirt, suspenders, and a pair of pinstripe pants, a comb tucked neatly in his pocket. It turned out he'd been visiting his boyfriend in Albany and had just got back. The tiny suitcase, affixed with stickers from all over the world, should have given it away. Gordon was dressed for court too, in a tweed coat and dark jeans, his hair was combed back and his beard was trimmed and he was still the handsomest man in town.

Johnny came out of the bathroom, smelling like bay rum. He said, I thought you weren't going to be staying here.

I'm not, I said.

Then Gordon said Chad was going to represent him in court.

I don't think that's a good idea, I said.

Oh no? said Johnny. You think we have a better advantage with a licensed pesticide handler by our side?

Chad's degree is in accounting, I said, pointing toward the baseboard.

Johnny fixed me with a blank look. Gordon picked Chad up from the floor and put him in his coat pocket.

Kylie, Gordon said in the car, remember when we went to the fair and convinced those people we were ticket takers? Then used their tickets to go on the Gravitron?

The memory scratched at something that hadn't been buried right.

Out the window, telephone poles were covered in kudzu. A heron stood at the edge of a reedy swamp, tall as a man. An acre of junked cars spread back into the land. And all the time the white sky burned down on us like the center of a soldering gun.

The courtroom had a drop ceiling and fluorescent lights and it smelled of Lysol and spit cups. DeChellis was there. People scraped their folding chairs along the linoleum when we walked in trying to get a look at Gordon. Their wet umbrellas leaned against the radiator steaming and their boots slicked the floor and I held Gordon's hand on reflex like he was walking me to school.

The couple's lawyer described how they had arrived home to find their terrier gone, then went out searching. When they came home Gordon and the dog were sitting in the living room watching television.

They were frightened by my uncle's size, the lawyer said. They were frightened because someone had affixed a little doll to their dog's back with scotch tape. They were frightened, he said, because next to Gordon on the couch were some "little mice with real fur."

As if there are other kinds of mice.

People started talking out loud.

The judge rapped the gavel and said there would be order. Then he looked up and his eyes lit upon mine and his face went pale.

Town Judge was an elected position in Burdett. His real job was wildlife manager for the county and the last time he'd seen me was just after my mother's body was found. Her body had been a great help to wildlife out there in the forest for a month and a half.

When I got back, Dechellis was sitting outside the double-wide on an upside-down milk crate, smoking and getting the rare sun on his face. Two men came out of the trailer with a nylon bag and some tent posts. They walked along the perimeter of the electric fence, nodding hello as they slipped down the embankment.

He'da got sent away if you hadn't been there, Dechellis told me. Order of Protection's nothing, just a slap on the wrist. But there you were to look at everyone with that memory of her face, and he goes right back to his house. All that space and all those rooms to your-selves. Nothing in them but tiny furniture and toy mice. Toy mice kept outta the cold. Toy mice sitting around the fire keeping warm, no mouths to eat, no noses to smell but he's cooking them food.

Christmas Wonderland glowed faintly in the afternoon light; its cables and wires laid bare.

I don't live up there anymore, I said scraping the bottom of my shoe on the cinderblock step. Inside my pocket I held Chad's cold hand between my finger and thumb.

That's why everyone loved you, Lollipop, DeChellis said. Just like your momma. You always knew to succeed was to fail.

THEY

They found the mouse's sister in the basement. She had lost a fingernail, and the skin beneath was blue. Her fur was patchy and oily-looking. Her brow furrowed; eyes focused on the middle distance, as if there was something she was trying to remember. The air was cool, dust motes circling in the air, suspended in a shaft of light. She sat on her hind legs, one hand tucked into her fur and the damaged one extended, a bruised finger pointing of its own volition toward the hurricane door.

The mouse himself was said to be living in a couch in the southern part of the city, working on a top-secret project that would turn snow into food.

When they found her, they brought her back behind the baseboard, said she'd missed two days of school. It was bad luck to ask where she'd been, so no one did. Her fur was hot, and her hands and feet were hot and her tongue was dry. Her expression had settled into a squint and it looked like she was about to remember, but she didn't.

She ate the orange peels they brought to her, and they said she must have been given messages, because she was hungry, and hunger is where messages and prayers came from. They thought she had become religious, because she ate now in answer to prayers.

No, I didn't pray for oranges, she told them wiping her mouth with the good hand, trying to focus on their faces. She rubbed her little finger against her gums.

Your brother is still working on the snow project, they told her. Whenever they said the word *snow* they whispered it. And she thought, listening to them, I will never whisper the word *snow* again. She knew this was true but didn't know why. I will never whisper *snow*, she thought. I will never whisper *dog*. I will never whisper *trap*. I will never whisper *cat*. I will never whisper *snake*. And it seemed like words were steps, were smells, and that she was walking up a little path that cooled her skin and wet her tongue as she got closer to the end of it. And she squinted harder to see what was at the end.

Were you given a message, then? they asked. And one of her sisters patted down her fur, the other took out a comb.

No, she said.

You can reveal it. And again, they whispered when they said the word *reveal*. I will never whisper *reveal*, the mouse's sister thought. I will never whisper *snake*. I will never whisper *cold*. I will never whisper *bird*.

Did you find some poison? they asked.

I will never whisper *poison*, she thought. Her skin felt cooler and she was getting closer to the end of the little path in her mind.

They left her behind the baseboard. They said, Tomorrow there is school. Her face was still set in brooding. Whatever it was she'd forgotten, she thought, she couldn't have known it by heart. She would keep chewing on it, like building the exit, first it's a wall then it's a space. You just keep chewing.

She sat on her hind legs, leaning against a pile of lint and cardboard tucked between the wall and an electrical cable. Her blue finger pointed down the long corridor, at little blades of light radiating in from around the nail heads like rays of a black-centered sun.

The schoolmaster didn't ask why she'd been gone because it was bad luck.

He said, this is what the air smells like beneath the tree where the owl sits. This is the number of stitches to cast on when you're knitting a cap. A great project is underway that will make us free. Your brothers are involved. They're risking themselves. They're making sacrifices in their standards of living.

When she left the classroom, the corridors smelled like something putrid and loamy. All around her she could smell it and she ran to the toilet to vomit. Her sisters were combing their hair in front of a strip of aluminum foil that hung above a row of square white sinks.

Are you okay? they asked.

Yes, the mouse's sister said. It's that smell in the hallway. Can't you smell it?

They turned their heads toward the door and raised their noses. We smell orange peel and stomach bile.

Can't you smell the other smell?

No, they said. Their shoelaces had pictures of cherries and strawberries on them.

The mouse's sister stood beside them and looked at the warped reflection of her face. She raised her hands to her whiskers and saw the crooked blue finger.

It's time to go, her sisters said. It's time to go to class. They put their combs in their school bags and left through the round door.

In the next class they watched a play. The mouse's sister dozed and felt hot. The play was about preparing for the snow project. Six mice wearing caps walked across a stage and three mice threw wood shavings into the air. One mouse pretended to be dead, and in the end, they ate the wood shavings. *Sacrifice for Freedom from Scarcity and Cold* was the name of the play. In her mind she shouted *scarcity* and then *cold*. And then *owl*. And the path opened before her in her fevered dreamy state, and her face reflected the stillness of one who is about to hear, about to be visited.

When had any of them felt cold? Or known scarcity? In her mind, a path raised up and she could not see beyond the crest of a little hill, but she thought she could almost make out the whiskers on the berries she was certain would grow there. Her fur felt wet; hot like she was living inside a stove. And she could faintly detect that smell again.

Snow, she thought, white and thick like a layer of fat, floating down to stiffen the world. There was nothing to fear in it. They lived inside the cut flesh of trees, gone dry and dead. And stones pressed together. All those things smelled different from the world, smelled like the idea for the snow project; paltry tattered visions born from hunger that made them alert, made them whisper.

All the things that came from nowhere were indisputable, like snow and air and rain. She did not want these things changed. She didn't want hunger to bring messages. She wanted to eat insects. She wanted to eat rye. The mouse's sister wanted snow and snakes and dogs and cold. Because, in the basement, she had seen the things that should be spoken about in a whisper.

———————

At once she could feel how the air in the basement was different than the air in the rest of the priory; close and cold, it told her fur to grow. She walked slowly, stretched up and listened, smelled the earth. She felt how the basement was the seed of the priory; all the other nests and the school owed something to it.

Something moved by the stone wall and she hurried toward it, stopping to sit and watch from behind a metal pole. There beneath a squat square of sunlight stood another mouse. He had captured a bee, tied it to a leash and was letting it fly up toward the square of light then jerking it back down to hit the floor. The thing was missing legs and its voice was hoarse from trying to reason with the mouse. Even from a distance she could feel its thirst.

This bee was the sole survivor of a group of brothers who strayed once they entered the priory by mistake. They had heard something in the basement, but it had turned out to be jars of jam. You can't dance directions to the sound of jars of jam, and so they'd tried to leave. The desiccated bodies of the bee's brothers lay half eaten near the wall beneath the squat square of light.

It's not right for you to eat them, she heard the bee tell the mouse. He hovered just before the mouse's face, waving his remaining legs in a frantic dance. I am to eat my brothers. My brothers are to eat my brothers. All of our children are to eat us. Not you. His tone revealed this was a speech he had been making for some time, his voice brittle as a dead leaf. And it seemed to the mouse's sister that he had lost his mind.

The mouse jerked the bee again and he bounced roughly off the floor. Our home is of our body, our food is of our body, the bee said, his voice cracking. We build from nothing. Each of us is one and all of us is one.

The mouse laughed; his eyes bulged like black mirrors, and the yellow reflection of the trapped bee moved over their surface like little flames flickering up from deep inside him.

You eat garbage, the bee went on, you are food. You are illness. Let us go. He waved his stinger about and the mouse's sister was certain now there was no sanity in his grief; being leashed by this mouse had destroyed him. He was the sole living bee and she wondered why the mouse didn't eat him or let him go. Why he didn't finish the other bees, which looked appetizing.

She moved quickly into his field of vision and stood silent, watching the bee struggle. And the mouse saw her and spoke to her with the kindest voice.

What are you doing down in the walled-off earth? he said, but his eyes still bulged and flickered with the bee's yellow reflection.

I go where I like, she told him. The bee was silent now, terrified.

Your brother is working on the snow project, isn't he?

Yes, she said.

I've been to that couch, he told her. I recognize your face. You look like him, you look like those who were called. They were from the same birth, but your brother has your exact face.

She nodded.

Let me go, the bee said.

In the couch, the mouse said, they are living on top of one another. They are breeding with mice that lived there for centuries. Those mice whisper every word they say, not just words like *fire*. I worked on that project myself.

He's insane as well, she thought, and eyed the bodies of the bees.

They are eating all their young as they are born, said the mouse. And they have learned a new language of shouts in which there is no word for snow.

Kill him, the bee shouted to the mouse's sister. But the mouse reeled the bee in and clutched him by his wings, holding him at arms-length before her. His eyes a black flame. I've been chained to him most of my life, said the bee, waving his remaining legs. All this, for what turned out to be jam.

Is your home really made from your body? the mouse's sister asked the bee.

He shook himself in exasperation. Kill him, he said again, Kill him.

Then all at once the mouse thrust the bee forward. She put her hand out to cover herself and the stinger shot through her palm, nailed her hand to the opposite shoulder. The mouse yanked the bee away, a husk now, its insides hanging down the front of her. And the silent shell of the sole bee was tossed to the floor still wearing its leash.

The flame vanished from the mouse's eyes, and they turned black and empty like holes.

It is they that are illness, the mouse said to her. It is they that are food, he said.

The bee venom put the mouse's sister to sleep. When she woke, she pulled the stinger out. She ate the bodies of the bee and his brothers. Then she stood watching the square of light grow and recede. Her hand swelled and her fingernail dropped off. And it was then she first smelled, but only faintly, that odor of something turning.

———————

She smelled it now at her desk. And didn't know how her sisters could breathe. Her hand had turned black and green and the finger burned. It had its own heart. It itched and was hot. She pressed it against the cool desktop, which offered only seconds of relief. Then scraped it against her teeth. And all the while the smell grew.

What did we learn from the play? The schoolmaster said.

We learned about sacrifice, her sisters said.

And what else? he asked, writing the word on the chalkboard. Food?

Yes, he wrote this as well. And what else?

There is a great threat of scarcity, they said. When he wrote this he abbreviated the words with a lowercase "t" and a lowercase "s."

They don't know the word for s-n-o-w anymore, the mouse's sister said.

No, but it does have to do with that word.

They are turning snow into food, one of the brightest sisters said.

Right. He wrote *food* on the chalkboard. Very good.

And they are breeding and then eating the young, the mouse's sister said, still scraping her finger against her teeth, because they have no room and have wed slave mice who only know how to speak in whispers.

No, said the schoolmaster, but they *are* making sacrifices in their standard of living.

I don't think my brother would want to father slave mice, she said. I think he'd eat them if he did.

It was bad luck to respond, so they spoke about paper bags, paper plates, and cake. She tried to walk up the little path in her mind again to soothe her bruised finger and cool her body. But she couldn't see it.

After school her sisters said, Why did you give those answers?

Can't you smell that? she asked.

No, they said.

She bit at the finger and a cold wire shot through her. She shuddered, then bit some more. It was all right. Her hand hurt. If it was gone it couldn't hurt. It was like building an exit.

Back behind the cupboard she leaned against the pile of lint and chewed at her blue hand until it was gone. Then she slept. When she woke, the smell was there behind the baseboards too. She watched the blades of light shining through the nail holes and felt no pain. A bone shone from inside the clean cut, and she tucked it into her fur.

At school her sisters said, Why have you eaten your hand?

It was painful, now it's gone.

How will you get on in your studies without it?

Can you smell that? she asked them.

We can't, they said, we can't.

They went to the bathroom and the mouse's sister watched them comb their hair; moving their hands, scraping the comb against their heads and faces. As if they were extracting something from inside themselves. Maybe this combing is how they get information. Maybe this combing brings the correct answers, the mouse's sister thought.

She pulled a handkerchief from her pocket and blew her nose. At this her sisters stopped their combing and raised their faces in her direction.

We can smell it now, they said.

Inside the handkerchief it was the color of blackberries and thick like molasses. And she gagged. This is the source of the smell, she said.

Yes. That is definitely the source of the smell, they said. And this time they whispered the word *smell*. It's time to go to, they said. It's time to go to class.

It was bad luck to speak about her missing hand, so the schoolmaster didn't. He said, Today we are listening to a choir. They are singing about the freedom that will soon be ours.

The choir was made up of older mice all wearing red blazers. Each of them could make their face look as though they had just found a sack of oats. I wonder if we'll get the oats after their song, the mouse's sister thought. The choirmaster held out a white wand, slender as the bone in her arm. It poked the air and they began to sing, and she saw that their eyes bulged like the eyes of the mouse in the basement, and that the wand moved inside their eyes like the reflection of the bee. The wand chopped and poked, duplicated in the sets of eyes. In the eyes of the choir, the wand was thin and sharp. In the eyes of the choir, it was a little white whip. They had the kindest voices, like the mouse in the basement.

She dozed as they sang, waking for the crescendos, for parts where they clapped their hands or stomped their feet.

One song was about a paper bag under a sink, and another was about feeding barley to the young. Another song was about not eating soap. Then there was a solo about some very soft insulation. The ending number was about the snow project, and they marched in place as they sang it.

When they finished, the choirmaster put the wand away and their eyes sank deeper into their heads and everyone clapped. The mouse's sister did not have to clap.

What did we learn from the songs? the schoolmaster asked later.

Insulation is good for nests, her sisters said.

Right, and what else?

We always need more food, they said. For the young, they added after a moment.

Right.

The best place to find a paper bag is under a sink.

Very good, the schoolmaster nodded.

Bees make both their homes and their food from nothing, said the mouse's sister.

No, the schoolmaster said. But there is the letter B in something we learned.

We have to *be* quiet, her sisters said.

Yes, Yes. Very good. What else?

We are food, the mouse's sister said. And we live by stealing. And the young taste very good.

It was bad luck to respond, so the schoolmaster ended the lesson by telling them that there were many more words that should be spoken in whispers. And that some whispered words didn't exist at all.

The mouse's sister blew more of the sticky substance out of her nose as she made her way back home. It smelled like a grave. Her face revealed that she was trying to remember something, and it was a mistake to have blown her nose because now it was running freely. Someone is building an exit, she said to herself. *Cold*, she shouted in her mind, leaning back on the electrical cable. *Scarcity, reveal, snow, trap, cat.* And she could no longer smell the grave coming from inside her. *Cake*, she whispered aloud. *Food*, she whispered, *grain.* And she could see again the little road in her mind. She could see beyond the crest of the hill. And there, just as she'd imagined, were berries. Each one made up of hundreds of little round sacs, and they had little whiskers growing in the cracks between. Each of them is one and all of them is one, she said to herself. And she felt a great thirst. Her eyes reflected only what was inside her head, and nothing else. Not a sole slave bee nor a white whip. Her eyes were flat black mirrors, raised so that they could never catch the look of one who passed by; one who passed, glancing for their own reflection. Her eyes calm and still like water, and she could see the road and the hedgerow of berries. *Dog*, she shouted. *Bird, snake*, she shouted. And she followed the little path backwards until it reached through the black-centered suns in the baseboard and ended at a pool of something dark and sticky she had been standing in. The little path came from nowhere right to her feet.

She left the ambry and made her way out to the rest of the priory, which was made from the silent insides of trees. She could still see the path. She ran and her white toes struck barely audible against the boards. She crossed through the center of the priory and saw her sister's faces each poking from their separate nests, their eyes shining.

Your brother has not returned from the project yet, they called to her. We will learn the songs to sing to him and to the other conscripts when we go to school.

She said nothing in reply, turned a corner, and followed alongside the baseboard until she reached a long strip of light as wide as her body and as tall as the priory. The long crack of light shone in her sister's eyes, curving over the surface of them.

You won't learn a thing inside that little sliver of light, they called to her as she slipped through it.

Something invisible ran itself over her body, like all the hands of her sisters pressing her fur down. Like an invisible comb that could comb everywhere at once. It pressed against her face and made itself minute and entered her nostrils. She opened her mouth and swallowed some of it. She saw her fur moving under the power of the invisible comb.

Dog, she shouted at the top of her lungs, *Dog, poison, owl, fire*. She pointed the stub of her right hand in the direction of the little hill. She could smell grain all around her, young grain and still water. She could smell the earth.

The voices of insects rose and the trees murmured and the dark syrup poured from her nose. It burst forth and she opened her mouth and let it flow from her as if all that was inside her was another mouse made of a liquid grave. That mouse couldn't live inside the crack of light. She would leave it on the doorstep of the priory.

Poison, Trap, Cat! she shouted. The last of the other mouse trickled from her nose and stuck to her fur and she began to run. She reached a hollow between the earth and the stump of a silent maple. The mouse's sister put her ear against his smooth roots, and saw hanging beside her, the gray blue thorns, and the hundreds of red sacs that made up the roundness of a berry.

Food, she whispered, raising herself up so that her whiskers brushed the whiskers of the berry. Food, she whispered, and filled her mouth with its blood.

ACKNOWLEDGMENTS

Jon Frankel read multiple drafts of these stories and of my novels, and has been my first reader and editor for more than twenty years. I'm grateful for his faith, humor, and generosity of spirit.

Deepest gratitude my comrades at PM Press, Ramsey Kanaan, Stephanie Pasvankias, Joey Paxman, Jonathan Rowland, Steven Stothard, Michael Ryan, Gregory Nipper, Dan Fedorenko, and Brian Layng. I wrote three of the stories in this collection in a studio at the Saltonstall Foundation. The story "RUIN" was part of a series I began at MacDowell and completed at the Edward Albee Foundation. I'm grateful to have had fellowships from these institutions. Thanks to *The Anarchist Review of Books* editorial collective—All power to the Imagination. Thank you Marc Lepson, artist, collaborator, friend, Σ'αγαπαω συντροφος μου. Thank you to Ann Godwin, Rebecca Friedman, Mattilda Bernstein Sycamore, Morgan Talty, Yasmin Nair, Nick Mamatas, Ben Durham, Mitchell Jackson, Katie Freeman, Panagiotis Kechagias, Corinne Manning, Carrie Laben and Peter Werbe for the conversations and clarity of vision, which helped me stay true to the intentions of this work. Thank you Maria Xilouri for making all the connections and for creating the most sanity-saving playlist a girl could listen to. Thanks to Ami Ben-Yaacov for insight and help with the research for *Strike Anywhere*, and for many other things over dozens of other years. Thank you to my loves E., Dh., and Em. Thank you to Herman "Poppy" Lepson, Dove "Woodward" Lepson, and Zane "Bernstein" Lepson. Thank you to my brothers and to my parents for their love, wit, and support. Mike Brutvan and Louise Felker navigated many miles of forest in fall, winter, and spring, leading expeditions through thick woods, deep snow and marsh, and talking all the while; Jesse and Michaela Schmidbauer showed me a new way to see a river I had known my whole life. Jamie Newman, Julie Blattberg and Lisa Chambers, the NYC H-group, dressed like modernist luminaries and wore flower wreaths and masks for a party I never thought I'd have. Thank you friends. Thanks to Joe Schmidbauer for providing a framework in which I could learn to write and think without academic interference and to Jack Goldman, who has always had the courage to champion radical work, and the taste to make it beautiful.

Thank you to P.P.O.W, the Estate of David Wojnarowicz, and Marion Scemama for graciously extending the rights to *Inside This Little House* for the cover of *RUIN*.

My eternal gratitude to Anneliis Beadnell. "We rise to greet the state, to confront the state. Smell the flowers while you can."

ABOUT THE AUTHOR

Cara Hoffman is the author of *Running*, a New York Times Editor's Choice, an *Esquire* magazine Best Book of the Year, and an *Autostraddle* Best Queer and Feminist Book of the Year. She first received national attention in 2011 with the publication of the feminist classic *So Much Pretty*, which sparked a national dialogue on violence and retribution and was named a Best Novel of the Year by the *New York Times Book Review*. Her second novel, *Be Safe I Love You*, was nominated for a Folio Prize and named one of the Five Best Modern War Novels by the *Telegraph* UK. She has written for the *New York Times, Paris Review, Bookforum, Bennington Review, Elle, The Daily Beast, Rolling Stone, Teen Vogue* and NPR and is a founding editor of *The Anarchist Review of Books*. A MacDowell Fellow and an Edward Albee Fellow, she has lectured at Oxford University's Rhodes Global Scholars Symposium. She lives in New York City and Athens, Greece.

ABOUT PM PRESS

PM Press is an independent, radical publisher of books and media to educate, entertain, and inspire. Founded in 2007 by a small group of people with decades of publishing, media, and organizing experience, PM Press amplifies the voices of radical authors, artists, and activists. Our aim is to deliver bold political ideas and vital stories to all walks of life and arm the dreamers to demand the impossible. We have sold millions of copies of our books, most often one at a time, face to face. We're old enough to know what we're doing and young enough to know what's at stake. Join us to create a better world.

PM Press
PO Box 23912
Oakland, CA 94623
www.pmpress.org

PM Press in Europe
europe@pmpress.org
www.pmpress.org.uk

FRIENDS OF PM PRESS

These are indisputably momentous times—the
financial system is melting down globally and the
Empire is stumbling. Now more than ever there is a
vital need for radical ideas.

In the years since its founding—and on a mere
shoestring—PM Press has risen to the formidable challenge of publishing and
distributing knowledge and entertainment for the struggles ahead. With over
450 releases to date, we have published an impressive and stimulating array
of literature, art, music, politics, and culture. Using every available medium,
we've succeeded in connecting those hungry for ideas and information to those
putting them into practice.

Friends of PM allows you to directly help impact, amplify, and revitalize the
discourse and actions of radical writers, filmmakers, and artists. It provides us
with a stable foundation from which we can build upon our early successes and
provides a much-needed subsidy for the materials that can't necessarily pay
their own way. You can help make that happen—and receive every new title
automatically delivered to your door once a month—by joining as a Friend of
PM Press. And, we'll throw in a free T-shirt when you sign up.

Here are your options:

- **$30 a month** Get all books and pamphlets plus 50% discount on all webstore
  purchases

- **$40 a month** Get all PM Press releases (including CDs and DVDs) plus 50%
  discount on all webstore purchases

- **$100 a month** Superstar—Everything plus PM merchandise, free downloads,
  and 50% discount on all webstore purchases

For those who can't afford $30 or more a month, we have **Sustainer Rates** at
$15, $10 and $5. Sustainers get a free PM Press T-shirt and a 50% discount on
all purchases from our website.

Your Visa or Mastercard will be billed once a month, until you tell us to stop.
Or until our efforts succeed in bringing the revolution around. Or the financial
meltdown of Capital makes plastic redundant. Whichever comes first.

God's Teeth and Other Phenomena

James Kelman

ISBN: 978-1-62963-939-0 (paperback)
      978-1-62963-940-6 (hardcover)
$17.95/$34.95   384 pages

Jack Proctor, a celebrated older writer and curmudgeon, goes off to residency where he is to be honored, teach and give public readings, he soon finds the atmosphere of the literary world has changed since his last foray into the public sphere. Unknown to most, unable to work on his own writing, surrounded by a host of odd characters, would-be writers, antagonists, handlers, and members of the elite House of Art and Aesthetics, Proctor finds himself driven to distraction (literally in a very very tiny car). This is a story of a man attempting not to go mad when forced to stop his own writing in order to coach others to write. Proctor's tour of rural places, pubs, theaters, fancy parties, where he is to be headlining as a "Banker-Prize-Winning-Author" reads like a literary version of *Spinal Tap*. Uproariously funny, brilliantly philosophical, gorgeously written this is James Kelman at his best.

James Kelman was born in Glasgow, June 1946, and left school in 1961. He travelled and worked various jobs, and while living in London began to write. In 1994 he won the Booker Prize for *How Late It Was, How Late*. His novel *A Disaffection* was shortlisted for the Booker Prize and won the James Tait Black Memorial Prize for Fiction in 1989. In 1998 Kelman was awarded the Glenfiddich Spirit of Scotland Award. His 2008 novel *Kieron Smith, Boy* won the Saltire Society's Book of the Year and the Scottish Arts Council Book of the Year. He lives in Glasgow with his wife Marie, who has supported his work since 1969.

"God's Teeth and other Phenomena *is electric. Forget all the rubbish you've been told about how to write, the requirements of the marketplace and the much vaunted 'readability' that is supposed to be sacrosanct. This is a book about how art gets made, its murky, obsessive, unedifying demands and the endless, sometimes hilarious, humiliations literary life inflicts on even its most successful names.*"
—Eimear McBride author of *A Girl is a Half-Formed Thing* and *The Lesser Bohemians*

We, the Children of Cats

Tomoyuki Hoshino
Translated by Brian Bergstrom

ISBN: 978-1-60486-591-2
$20.00   288 pages

A man and woman find their genders and sexualities brought radically into question when their bodies sprout new parts, seemingly out of thin air. . . . A man travels from Japan to Latin America in search of revolutionary purpose and finds much more than he bargains for. . . . A journalist investigates a poisoning at an elementary school and gets lost in an underworld of buried crimes, secret societies, and haunted forests. . . . Two young killers, exiled from Japan, find a new beginning as resistance fighters in Peru. . . .

These are but a few of the stories told in *We, the Children of Cats*, a new collection of provocative early works by Tomoyuki Hoshino, winner of the 2011 Kenzaburo Oe Award in Literature and author of the powerhouse novel *Lonely Hearts Killer* (PM Press, 2009). Drawing on sources as diverse as Borges, Nabokov, Garcia-Marquez, Kenji Nakagami and traditional Japanese folklore, Hoshino creates a challenging, slyly subversive literary world all his own. By turns teasing and terrifying, laconic and luminous, the stories in this anthology demonstrate Hoshino's view of literature as "an art that wavers, like a heat shimmer, between joy at the prospect of becoming something else and despair at knowing that such a transformation is ultimately impossible . . . a novel's words trace the pattern of scars left by the struggle between these two feelings." Blending an uncompromising ethical vision with exuberant, freewheeling imagery and bracing formal experimentation, the five short stories and three novellas included in *We, the Children of Cats* show the full range and force of Hoshino's imagination; the anthology also includes an afterword by translator and editor Brian Bergstrom and a new preface by Hoshino himself.

"These wonderful stories make you laugh and cry, but mostly they astonish, co-mingling daily reality with the envelope pushed to the max and the interstice of the hard edges of life with the profoundly gentle ones."
—Helen Mitsios, editor of *New Japanese Voices: The Best Contemporary Fiction from Japan* and *Digital Geishas and Talking Frogs: The Best 21st Century Short Stories from Japan*

Late in the Day:
Poems 2010-2014
Ursula K. Le Guin

ISBN: 978-1-62963-122-6
$21.95   112 pages

Late in the Day, Ursula K. Le Guin's new collection of poems, seeks meaning in an ever-connected world. In part evocative of Neruda's *Odes to Common Things* and Mary Oliver's poetic guides to the natural world, Le Guin gives voice to objects that may not speak a human language but communicate with us nevertheless through and about the seasonal rhythms of the earth, the minute and the vast, the ordinary and the mythological.

As Le Guin herself states, "science explicates, poetry implicates." Accordingly, this immersive, tender collection implicates us (in the best sense) in a subjectivity of everyday objects and occurrences. Deceptively simple in form, the poems stand as an invitation both to dive deep and to step outside of ourselves and our common narratives. As readers, we emerge refreshed, having peered underneath cultural constructs toward the necessarily mystical and elemental, no matter how late in the day.

These poems of the last five years are bookended with two short essays, "Deep in Admiration" and "Form, Free Verse, Free Form: Some Thoughts."

"A life-long observer of humanity and nature, who has borne critical witness to over eighty years of the modern age."
—Jillian Saucier, *Rattle*

"She never loses touch with her reverence for the immense what is."
—Margaret Atwood

"There is no writer with an imagination as forceful and delicate as Ursula K. Le Guin's."
—Grace Paley

"Le Guin's down-to-earth, intensely personal voice is unmistakable."
—*Los Angeles Times*

Nazaré

JJ Amaworo Wilson

ISBN: 978-1-62963-908-6 (paperback)
978-1-62963-920-8 (hardcover)
$16.95/$24.95   320 pages

Nazaré: the great wave. Kin, an orphan scavenger in the Fishing Village with No Name, finds a stranded whale on the beach and tries to return it to the ocean. His efforts attract the attention of Mayor Matanza and his bloodthirsty police, the Tonto Macoute, and Kin must leave the only home he's ever known. His journeys take him to an abandoned lighthouse, through singing caves and brutal deserts, and finally to a village of warrior historians.

There he meets the Professor and others who are preparing to overthrow Matanza. They are joined by Jesa, a woman from Kin's village who might be a witch, and the nun Iquique. Their revolution is unlike any other, fought by tinkers and miners, monks and acrobats, clairvoyants in bowler hats, a painted saint, the King of the Rats, and a giant turtle named Abacaxi. The holy man Fundogu once told Kin, "You will do battle with monsters and you will do battle with men." As Fundogu's prophecy takes shape around him, Kin remembers another of Fundogu's sayings: "Everything begins and ends in the sea"

"I celebrate this novel for its sea village textures, its power-driven tides of story and characters, shaped and painted as if they were figures rising up from the buried truths of an ancient ocean and its peoples. The materials are multilayered with whale skin, song names, the breath of brujas and the whispers of old men and widowed women. There is tenderness, transcendence and the voyages into the unknown we all seek to enter and be reborn. Amaworo Wilson's dexterity, abundant materials, culture lens, and visual genius give us a rare, ground-shaking novel, a tidal wave of prizes."
—Juan Felipe Herrera, United States Poet Laureate

"Nazaré grabs the reader from the first page and never lets go, bringing us into so many rich and colorful worlds. This brilliant novel will earn JJ Amaworo Wilson a spotlight on the main stage of world fiction."
—Daniel Chacón, American Book Award winner, author of *Kafka in a Skirt*

The Cost of Lunch, Etc.

Marge Piercy

ISBN: 978-1-62963-125-7 (paperback)
**   978-1-60486-496-0 (hardcover)**
$15.95/$21.95   192 pages

Marge Piercy's debut collection of short stories, *The Cost of Lunch, Etc.*, brings us glimpses into the lives of everyday women moving through and making sense of their daily internal and external worlds. Keeping to the engaging, accessible language of Piercy's novels, the collection spans decades of her writing along with a range of locations, ages, and emotional states of her protagonists. From the first-person account of hoarding ("Saving Mother from Herself") to a girl's narrative of sexual and spiritual discovery ("Going over Jordan") to a recount of a past love affair ("The Easy Arrangement") each story is a tangible, vivid snapshot in a varied and subtly curated gallery of work. Whether grappling with death, familial relationships, friendship, sex, illness, or religion, Piercy's writing is as passionate, lucid, insightful, and thoughtfully alive as ever.

"The author displays an old-fashioned narrative drive and a set of well-realized characters permitted to lead their own believably odd lives."
—Thomas Mallon, *Newsday*

"This reviewer knows no other writer with Piercy's gifts for tracing the emotional route that two people take to a double bed, and the mental games and gambits each transacts there."
—Ron Grossman, *Chicago Tribune*

"Marge Piercy is not just an author, she's a cultural touchstone. Few writers in modern memory have sustained her passion, and skill, for creating stories of consequence."
—*Boston Globe*

"What Piercy has that Danielle Steel, for example, does not is an ability to capture life's complex texture, to chart shifting relationships and evolving consciousness within the context of political and economic realities she delineates with mordant matter-of-factness. Working within the venerable tradition of socially conscious fiction, she brings to it a feminist understanding of the impact such things as class and money have on personal interactions without ever losing sight of the crucial role played by individuals' responses to those things."
—Wendy Smith, *Chicago Sun-Times*